A Mother to Embarrass Me

OTHER DELL YEARLING BOOKS YOU WILL ENJOY

MY ANGELICA
Carol Lynch Williams

IF I FORGET, YOU REMEMBER
Carol Lynch Williams

THE TRUE COLORS OF CAITLYNNE JACKSON
Carol Lynch Williams

A NECKLACE OF RAINDROPS
Joan Aiken

MELANIE MARTIN GOES DUTCH
Carol Weston

TYLER ON PRIME TIME
Steve Atinsky

THE VICTORY GARDEN
Lee Kochenderfer

ALL THE WAY HOME
Patricia Reilly Giff

GROVER G. GRAHAM AND ME
Mary Quattlebaum

SOME KIND OF PRIDE
Maria Testa

DELL YEARLING BOOKS are designed especially to entertain and enlighten young people. Patricia Reilly Giff, consultant to this series, received her bachelor's degree from Marymount College and a master's degree in history from St. John's University. She holds a Professional Diploma in Reading and a Doctorate of Humane Letters from Hofstra University. She was a teacher and reading consultant for many years, and is the author of numerous books for young readers.

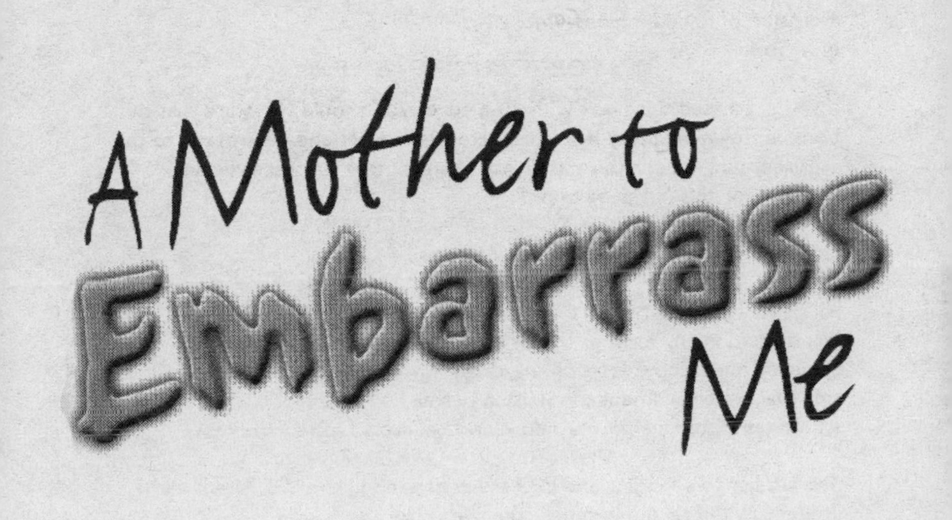

CAROL LYNCH WILLIAMS

A DELL YEARLING BOOK

Published by
Dell Yearling
an imprint of
Random House Children's Books
a division of Random House, Inc.
New York

Visit us on the Web! www.randomhouse.com/kids

Educators and librarians, for a variety of teaching tools, visit us at www.randomhouse.com/teachers

---

ISBN: 0-440-41810-0

Reprinted by arrangement with Delacorte Press

Printed in the United States of America

August 2003

10 9 8 7 6 5 4 3 2

OPM

Special thanks to Gary Price and
Dan Hildreth, famous sculptors,
who spent hours answering my questions

Dedicated to
Elise, Laura, Kyra, Caitlynne and Carolina,
my sweet, and many times embarrassed, daughters

The Mother

I wasn't even all the way home and I could hear it. Music. Old-timey music. Music that a lady almost forty would listen to. It was the Beatles, their "Twist and Shout" song, blasting so loud from my house that in my imagination I could see the curtains straining at the screens to get away from the sound.

I heaved a sigh and shifted my pile of library books from one hip to the other.

"Mom," I said under my breath. My voice came out a growl.

Here it was, the second day into summer vacation, and already there was trouble with my mother.

I turned the corner onto Maple Drive and looked in the direction of my place.

And that's when I saw him. Quinn Sumsion,

probably one of the best-looking guys I know. Probably one of the best-looking guys *anyone* knows. He walked toward me, his younger brother, Christian, in tow. They bounced a yellow-and-purple basketball between them, taking turns.

All of a sudden my books seemed sweaty and heavy. My face turned red. I wiped at my brow with my free hand and pretended I had never been more interested in a purple-and-yellow basketball.

The three of us were close enough now that I knew if I looked straight into his face, I'd see how blue Quinn's eyes were. I couldn't look, though. I mean, there was that basketball. And the music blasting from my house. And all these books I was carrying.

"Hey, Laura." It was Christian. He gave me a small smile, his braces catching just a glint of sunlight, then passed the ball to his brother.

"Hey," I said. I allowed myself a peek at Quinn. I moved a bit to the right and, without meaning to, stepped off the sidewalk with one foot. Three books skidded from the top of my pile and landed faceup on the sidewalk. One was called *The Dummies' Guidebook to Falling in Love.* I sucked in a breath of air through my nose and resisted the urge to kick this traitor book into the gutter, or to cover the title with my foot.

"Oopsie," I said. I hadn't thought it possible

for my face to get redder than it was. Why oh why couldn't something different have fallen? Why not *Lord of the Flies*? I went into a crouch and tried to pick things up. Christian bent too and scooped the books together, then heaped them back on for me.

Quinn bounced the ball, and from where I knelt I saw dirt puff up from the ground like a tiny explosion. "You gonna read all summer?" he asked. But he didn't wait for an answer. "I can't believe anyone would waste a summer reading."

"I read every summer," I said, not looking at him. My gosh, he was talking to me. To me!

"My brother—the big fat brain," Christian said. He tried to steal the ball from Quinn but missed, and his hand swiped at air.

"College coming up," Quinn said, twisting from Christian. "I want to have some fun before I start grinding away at learning. I want to rest my brain." He dribbled the basketball, allowing it to bounce in a figure eight while he stepped around it.

You are the cutest thing I have ever seen in my life, I thought. My brain shouted these words. I could have stood there all the rest of the summer, holding my ninety-pound stack of books and staring at Quinn Sumsion.

Quinn nodded a little, almost like he knew my thoughts.

"I can hear your mom's working," he said.

"Uh," I said. I think I might have said more, at this one chance to talk to him, but right then, at that very moment, Mom began to yodel. It's this thing she does with her voice every time she sings with an old-fart song like the one that was on now. She finds a harmony and sings it louder than anyone without a microphone should be able to do.

"Twist it, baby," Mom sang. "Twist it this way and that way and this way. Come on, baaa-bee. Shout, shout, shout." She was making up her own words. She always makes up her own words.

I couldn't look at Quinn when the yodeling began. I couldn't even look at Christian, and he and I have been friends since third grade. All I could do was pin my sights on my front door, which stood wide open, and walk fast toward home. "Gotta go," I said.

I planned on jerking that Beatles *Anthology* CD out of the player and slinging it to Kingdom Come, a place my father is always talking about.

"A little game later?" Christian asked me. From the corner of my eye I saw him steal the ball from Quinn, who put his hands in his pockets like he meant for that to happen. Then Christian twirled the ball, trying to make it spin on his finger the way those guys on TV do.

"Sure," I said. "Maybe. I gotta get this stuff home." My voice came out almost whiny, the way it sounds when Mom gets on my nerves and

I want her to stop something. Lately that's been everything she does. She embarrasses me more than should be allowed. This was a perfect example.

I pushed past the Sumsion brothers and, with my face burning with shame, tried to run the half block home, which isn't so easy when you're carrying as many books as I was. Lucky for me nothing else fell, including myself.

"Hey, Laura," Quinn called again.

I turned, slowing my flight, hoping my face didn't appear as bright as it felt. I tried to swallow a big glob of spit as Mom belted out, "Do it, do it, do it, sweet thing."

"Tell your mom she's got a great set of lungs." Then he laughed.

I nodded a little and opened my mouth to answer him, but no real sound came out. I tried to hold my head high as I left. But I couldn't. It was like I felt myself folding up: my shoulders moving closer to the books, moving closer to my stomach, moving closer to my toes. I was curling up like a potato bug.

"Mom," I whispered toward my belly button. "Mom." Only what more could I say after that? I needed a plan. I needed control. I was on the front porch now, the wraparound porch that reminds Mom of Florida. I needed the music off to think.

I pulled open the screen door and closed the

solid wood door behind me. Maybe that would block some of the sound. I peeked out the side window, allowing only one eyeball to look. Christian stood gazing at my house. Quinn walked down the street away from his brother. Away from me. Away from my heart. I fell back against the wall and clutched at my chest.

"Oh, I love him. I love him," I whispered. At least I think I whispered those deep and pained words. Really it was hard to tell, what with the music so loud.

This music! I made my way to the stairs. I took them two at a time up to my bedroom, where I piled the library books next to my desk.

Mom must be in her front-room office, probably drawing. She always listens to music this loud when she's designing something. Or else she was sculpting in her studio. The "work" Quinn had suggested.

There was a moment of silence when "Twist and Shout" finished. It seemed the whole house breathed a sigh of relief. I know I did. No more music, maybe. I wrinkled my forehead, hoping. Then came the huge sound of someone snapping his fingers and Billy Squier was singing, Mom accompanying him, to "Rock Me Tonight."

I slammed my door hard. The bedroom floor vibrated with what Mom called one of her favorite dance songs.

"Jeez, Mom," I hollered through the closed

door. "Give it a rest. The least you could do is listen to good stuff." The stuff that was on the radio. The stuff *real* people listened to. But she didn't hear me. How was it possible with Billy Squier nearly rocking our home off its foundation? Wasn't it bad enough that I knew all the olden-day singers because of her? I was probably the only kid in the world that did. It wasn't fair.

I went over to the window and looked out at the back two acres that we call our land. This two acres, no, all of Mapleton, Utah, didn't seem big enough to hide Mom.

I had to think of a way to change her.

On the nightstand next to my bed was a slip of paper. I had lots of these, which I would later staple onto a page in my journal. On them I wrote lists. One list was of my favorite books (that one was really long), one was of who I thought was cute (that one was short—Quinn Sumsion), one was of dreams of what I'd do if I had two million dollars. I started another. "Things to change about MY MOTHER." I underlined it three times and had about ten exclamation points following the title.

I was ready.

Complete Overhaul Needed

I lay in bed for a long time staring at the ceiling. It seems that for all my life Mom has been embarrassing the heck out of me, but I know that isn't quite true. Not when I really think about it. I mean, only last year I can remember being *proud* of Mom.

Mary Wolf, one of my best friends, and I shared fifth grade. She lives only two doors down from Quinn and Christian. That makes it easy for me to walk by Quinn's house, what with him living so close to Mary.

Anyway, she and I sat side by side, right in the front of Mr. Bennion's fifth-grade class. It was there, sneaking notes to each other, that we became friends.

And it was Mr. Bennion who had parents come and visit our class and tell what they did for their job. I think it was some career day thing.

Derek Larson's mom talked about being a three-dimensional artist. She showed a couple of her paintings, complete with doors you could open and close.

Allie Keene's dad talked about being an inventor. He showed a pager that he had worked on that showed all kinds of important information on it, like when your next appointment was and where.

Mary's mom is a stay-at-home mom. She brought in jars of food she had canned and a loaf of fresh bread that was still warm and even a great big carrot cake for everyone to try.

Then in came my mother, dressed in her work clothes, a pair of blue jeans and an old T-shirt. Now, at the memory, I shivered with embarrassment. Why did she wear those clothes, spattered with paint and smeared with clay, to school that day? And why hadn't it bothered me then? Like it did now. It could have been worse, I knew that. Sometimes Mom works in her pajamas.

Anyway, I remember she held up a sculpture she was working on, one that she called *Freedom*. It was a little girl, her hair blowing forward, holding on to a kite that really seemed to tug from the girl's hand.

"I modeled for that," I had whispered to Mary. And she said, "Wow, that's cool, Laura."

I hadn't been embarrassed of Mom then. In fact, I was so full of pride that day that when she came to sit in the back of the room with the other parents, I grinned big at her. She grinned back and I felt this big gush of love. So big that I actually wanted to hug her. In public. In my classroom, of all things. Right in front of everybody.

I shivered again, glad that I hadn't been so stupid that day to do something like hug my mother in front of other people.

So when had the change happened, this being embarrassed? It almost seemed an overnight thing that Mom went from cool to geek. How could anyone change so fast?

I looked at my list. My mother-changing list. The list that just might succeed in making me the happiest woman alive. Right at the moment I felt like a woman. Not just a twelve-year-old. I felt like a woman with a list waiting to emerge from her fingertips—well, really the pencil I held in my fingertips—to fall upon—well, really write—the things that would set my mother straight. Forever.

I needed a hundred pages of suggestions to make her an acceptable mother. Hundreds. This task before me was huge, one I felt only a woman could undertake. A twelve-year-old woman.

With great sincerity I wrote a large number one. I took my time, coloring around the edges with a gel pen.

Next to the number one I wrote: "Complete overhaul needed."

Just what would a complete overhaul take? Brain surgery? Did we have money for that? I was sure we did. In fact, I knew Mom and Dad had a college fund for me. Would they let me use it for something that might make me truly, truly happy?

"Start with something easier," I said out loud. "Something Mom could do if I helped her set her mind to it Something "

At that moment Mom's voice pierced through my door like a javelin might. "My baaa-bee." These two words were repeated many times.

Okay, number two on the list was easy.

2. her awful singing

So was number three.

3. her awful singing that is so loud all the world can hear

And four.

4. her awful, loud music

I stopped. Where were all the ideas now? All I had thought of were music-related items. But could I be blamed? Even a jury from *Ally McBeal* would agree with me that no human mind could think of anything more with that music blaring away.

Fine. I knew how to end the list. I turned five pages ahead in my notebook. At the bottom of the fifth page I wrote the number 100 and spelled out in careful, neat letters, "Change her whole mother self." I could fill in the rest as it came to me.

Mom was in the kitchen below, I could tell by her voice. She was singing again, this time making up the words to "Rock Me Tonight," along with a harmony that no one would recognize even fitted the song. Without going down there, I knew what she was doing. Dancing. Swinging her hips and hopping around on the stone kitchen floor, probably getting ready to start Dad's dinner.

"How much more of this can I take?" I asked the ceiling, where I had pinned a poster with the words WHO YOU ARE IS IMPORTANT, complete with a rainbow and a wrinkled-looking dog who didn't know how ugly he was.

I flung myself off my bed and stomped to my door. I threw it open wide, hard. It bounced against the wall, leaving a tiny ding.

"Mom," I shouted. "Mo-om." Anger warmed my cheeks. "Turn down the music."

Right at that moment the music stopped. "What's that, Laurie?" Mom sang the words, using another new tune. For sure she was in what she calls a "creative mode." All this singing proved that.

"It's Laura," I shouted. Why in the heck can't she even get my name right? "Can you please turn down the music?"

There was a moment of silence and then Mom said, "All right, honey."

"Thank you." I used my most sarcastic voice, then slammed the door shut for good measure. I plopped onto the bed again and for a moment felt a bit of satisfaction. Things stayed quiet downstairs. There was no music at all. I smiled to myself.

Mom's last words, "All right, honey," played back in my head. Guilt crept in around the edges of my satisfied feeling. Guilt! As if *I* should feel guilty about anything. Mom had embarrassed *me*. I had a right to be angry with her. Why did this guilt thing always happen to me? Why not to her?

"Fine," I said. "Just fine." I got up and stomped to my door and opened it. Mom wasn't going to win the battle without a fight.

I could hear the sounds of dishes being clinked together. I made my way to where Mom worked in the kitchen. She looked up when I came into the room.

"Hey, baby," she said. She looked worse than the day when she visited my classroom. She wore an old pair of blue-and-green flannel pajamas even though the sun was high in the sky. They're four inches too short and they bag in the butt. These are jammies that she doesn't sleep in but works in. In fact, she doesn't sleep in anything at all, a thing that has always embarrassed me, since before my birth, I'm sure.

"I like to be comfortable when I'm creating," she tells people who come to the door and see her in nightclothes.

"Did you find anything good at the library?" Mom asked.

I didn't answer for a second, then with an icy voice I spoke. "Yes." I looked in the fridge even though I wasn't interested in anything, a little amazed at how only one word could seem to mean so much.

But Mom didn't even notice my strong yes. "How about grilled cheese sandwiches for dinner tonight? I'm craving something fried." She didn't wait for me to answer. "I know I shouldn't, but I'm going to anyway."

I glanced at my mother with only one eye. It wasn't easy to do, even with the practice I had had at my front door, when I had looked out at Quinn and Christian. It wasn't easy to look at her, I mean, without really looking. From this position I could see that her cheeks were plump.

A little shock tremor went through my bones. I jerked my head around to get a full-on view. I nearly dislocated my neck in the process. Mother was a little . . . well, a nice word for it would be *chubby*.

"I'm working on a new piece," she said.

Shock had frozen my tongue. My skinny mother, bulging. When in the world had that happened? While I was at the library?

There was a knock at the door. Still I stood, staring at my mother with both eyes now.

"Would you get that, Laurie?"

I wanted to say yes but I couldn't. Instead I turned and walked toward the front door. I felt like a zombie, only slower. Mother—fat. My mother, fat. My mother, ex-model turned sculptor, fat. It was enough to make a crazed man sane.

FAT?

It was Mary at the door.

"You're back," she said, and then walked into the house. "I called you thirty-eight times and there was no answer. Check caller ID if you don't believe me." Her hair was braided in lots of tiny braids with beads at the ends. Mary's older sister, Karen, wants to be a beautician. She's always doing cool things to Mary's hair. I'd let her do cool things to mine, too, but Dad likes my hair the way it is 'cause it looks so much like Mom's.

"I believe you," I said, awakened from my zombie-like state.

"Did you get any good books?"

I nodded. "Yeah, I got that Richard Peck one you told me to read, about the *Titanic.*" Mary loves all of Richard Peck's books. Each of us always tells the other what titles are good. This summer we decided to see how many we could read before school starts again. My goal is one hundred.

"I came over to see if you wanted to walk to the library with me." Mary swung her head, and the little beads clinked together.

"Sure," I said. "I don't think Mom would care. Just as long as I'm home in time for dinner. She's actually making food tonight. We're not going out." I rolled my eyes in an exaggerated way and Mary laughed.

"I wish we were always going out to eat," she said.

"No you don't. After a while it gets boring. There aren't that many restaurants in our area." To tell you the truth, we'd have to be in a city bigger than New York to have enough variety, that's how much we eat out.

"Let's see if you can go," Mary said.

I grabbed her by the arm to stop her. "Do me a favor," I said, lowering my voice to a whisper. "See if Mom looks different to you."

"Different how?"

I noticed that the beads in Mary's hair matched the ties on her braces. "Different, different." I couldn't bring myself to say the word *fat*.

She gave me a squinch-eyed look, then said, "Okay."

We went into the kitchen. Sun splashed

through the windows onto the sink and countertops.

"Mare-Mare," Mom said in a voice that made it sound like she hadn't seen my friend in a million years and not just since yesterday. "Hello!" My mother is so cheerful that, sometimes, even *that* gets on my nerves.

"Hey, Mrs. Stephan. Can Laura go to the library with me? I'm out of books."

Mom had piled all the ingredients near the stove to make grilled cheese sandwiches: bread, cheese, butter, and a cookbook. A *cookbook*. Whoever heard of having to read directions on making a grilled cheese?

"We're having grilled cheese sandwiches for dinner. Chips, too," Mom said. She held up a package of Baked Lay's potato chips. "With fresh sour cream."

Good grief, I thought. I crossed my eyes at Mary, who ignored me and smiled at my mother.

Mom popped open the sour cream container and dipped her finger into it. She licked off the sour cream, then said, "Sure, Laurie can go. Can you two be back in an hour?"

Mary nodded and I heard the beads tap.

"By six o'clock, Laurie girl?"

"Okay," I said. Grrr. Laurie girl. I'd have to add nicknames to my list of things to change about my mother. And cheerfulness.

Mom came near to give me a kiss. She had a tiny bit of sour cream on her top lip. I wasn't sure if it was there by accident or if she had left it there on purpose. Sometimes she does that. I mean, sometimes she coats her lips with chocolate from-the-can icing and walks around like it's lipstick. That makes Dad laugh. It makes me sick. At least nowadays. It used to be I'd wear chocolate lipstick too. Now I've grown up. Too bad my mom hasn't.

"Let's go," I said, avoiding even looking at Mom. I hurried down the hall and out into the hot day.

"Well?" I said when we were out of hearing distance. Not that Mom would have heard. We weren't five steps out of the house when the Pointer Sisters' "I'm So Excited" came blasting out behind us.

"She looked fine to me. Beautiful as usual."

"Are you sure she didn't look . . ." Again I couldn't say *fat.*

"She looked as gorgeous as your mother always looks," Mary said. "It must be cool to have a mother who used to be a model."

"Not really," I said. "What's really cool is a mom who cleans the house and makes more than three kinds of meals and doesn't wear her pajamas to work in."

Mary laughed. These past few months we've

talked about this very thing a million times. She wishes her mom were more glamorous and I wish my mom were more normal.

"But she's in all those magazines."

It's true. Before Mom married Dad she was a high-fashion New York model. No lie. She's been on the cover of *Elle, Glamour, Cosmo* and a bunch of others. Mom saved everything in books she calls her portfolio in case she wants to go into modeling again. This includes all the last articles about when she decided to give up her exciting career to marry a Utah computer geek and settle down in the little town of Mapleton and start having babies.

The trouble is Mom was only able to have one baby: me. All her other pregnancies ended in miscarriages. Finally she and Dad quit trying.

"Let's talk books," I said, "not mothers."

"That's all right with me," Mary said. And that's what we did. We spent the rest of that hour walking and talking about books, then finding great books to read. We chatted with Vivian, our librarian, about what she liked to read, and with Pat, too. They both love kids' books. I even brought home a few more to add to my stack.

But before I began any reading, before I began *anything,* I would have to add a few more items to the list about changing Mom. And spy on her about this fat thing.

things to change about MY MOTHER!!!!!!!

5. *her always being happy*
6. *food on her face*
7. *working in her pajamas*
8. *Fat!?!*

Burning Down the House

There was a fire engine in front of the house when Mary and I got home. And one police car, its lights flashing blue. A crowd had gathered on our front lawn and neighbors stood in their own yards watching our place.

Mom waited on the front porch. Inside the house I could see smoke. It rolled out the door, dark and scary-looking. A lump came up into my throat and fear made my skin prickle.

"Oh my gosh," Mary said. "Laura, oh my gosh."

I couldn't say anything.

We started running, Mary with all her books and me with my five new ones, all Richard Peck paperbacks, thank goodness. It seemed I ran in slow motion. I couldn't get to Mom fast enough.

Once I almost fell, running through a small dip Dad landscaped into the yard so things would have a rolly, country look. Imagine that, us living in the country and all, and he wants to make sure it has a rustic feel. I've heard him say that. And now his designing slowed me down.

At last I was there, standing on the sidewalk that cuts the yard into sections, just a few feet away from my mother. I could hear Mom talking to the one policeman and all three firemen.

"I'm so sorry," she was saying. "I just went into my studio for a moment." She shrugged and pouted, pursing her lips. She looked quite beautiful, if not a little chubby, standing there with her arms crossed in front of her. I felt happy she wasn't still in her work pajamas. She must have changed because Dad was coming home.

One of the firemen, dressed in a dark blue shirt and thick yellow pants, smiled at Mom. "It's okay, Mrs. Stephan. That's what we're here for: to help."

The other two firemen nodded in agreement. So did the policeman. Everybody smiled. Except me. I could see what Mom was doing without her even meaning to: being a pretty woman. And all the men on our front porch were falling for it. Her pretty face, I mean. And her used-to-be-slim body. I wouldn't be at all surprised if they gave Mom a salute.

Mom saw me where I stood on the sidewalk. "Oh, Laurie," she said. For a moment I thought she might cry. Then she bit her bottom lip and gave me a brilliant smile.

"What happened?" I asked. I walked up to Mom and half the Mapleton, Utah, rescue team. Mary followed. "Did the kitchen burn up? Did our house catch on fire?" I was afraid to hear what my mother had to say. There was all the black smoke, after all.

Mom gave a nervous giggle. "Well, Laurie girl. I started cooking because Daddy will be home any minute. And while I was toasting the bread for grilled cheese, it happened. I used the whole loaf because I could tell this was going to be a fantastic dinner and I knew we'd all want seconds and maybe even thirds. I had just put the bread under the broiler for a moment, laid out all those pieces of pretty white—when it hit me."

The policeman smiled.

"What hit you, Mom?"

"Well." Mom shrugged a little again. "Well, I guess I feel creative when I cook because I all of the sudden had this idea for the piece I'm working on." Mom talked to everyone now. Not just to me.

I squeezed my eyes shut, somehow knowing what she was going to say. "Never mind," I said under my breath. "Never mind, Mom. I think I—"

Mom didn't hear, I guess, because she kept right on going. And everyone on the porch kept right on smiling. "So I went into the studio and started making a few minor adjustments."

"Mom." I could feel my face getting hot. "Why were you toasting things in the oven when you were going to brown the bread on the grill? You didn't need to toast it too."

Mom's head tilted like a little bird's. "I didn't?"

"Mom." I leaned close to her and she put her head on my shoulder. "You don't pretoast the bread. Everyone knows that. You just cook it. In a pan. On a grill."

"Now, Laurie girl," Mom said. "I haven't had that much experience in cooking yet and I got this idea and I wanted things to be nice for you and a little extra toasting seemed the smart thing to do . . ."

"Grrr," I said, "you could have burned the whole house up, Mom. I don't think you should use the broiler again. Ever." I looked at the policeman for support. He frowned at me.

"Jimmey!" Dad's voice came rolling over the lawn from the car window. He stopped his Jeep with a jerk after screeching into the driveway and nearly threw himself to the ground trying to get out. At least I think he might have thrown himself to the ground. He had forgotten to unfasten his seat belt, though. I watched, horrified, while he wrestled around in the front seat, trying to free himself. So did fifty other Mapleton residents. Including Quinn Sumsion, who stood on the edge of the crowd with Christian.

Dad's arms paddled around like he was slapping at kitchen smoke. His left leg was out of the car and it looked like he was riding a bike, the way he pedaled at the air. At last, one hand grasped at the lip of the door. He tried to pull himself free. All the while he called Mom's name: "Jimmey!"

Mom stopped her explanations, then started for my father, calling his name. "Danny, oh, Danny. I've done another bad thing." Her thick blond hair had fallen loose from the haphazard knot she'd pulled it into. For a moment I hoped she'd crawl over Dad and into the passenger seat and they'd drive out of town forever. My face burned as I watched the two of them.

Instead, she unbuckled my father. The whole crowd observed my crazy parents as Dad got out of the car and Mom slung her arms around his neck. Someone started clapping, and the next thing I knew, Mom was crying and waving and Dad was giving a small bow to this local ovation. Even the rescue team clapped.

Another fireman came out of the house and in a loud voice announced, "Mrs. Stephan, there's not even any smoke damage. You are one lucky woman."

The crowd applauded harder, and I heard the policeman say to no one in particular, "No, *Dan Stephan* is one lucky man."

I looked at Mary. "Stop clapping," I hissed at her.

She just grinned at me and pounded her hands harder. "Don't be a moron," she said.

I tried not to see Quinn Sumsion, but there he was, at the edge of the driveway, clapping for Mom and Dad too. So was Christian.

I turned and ran into the house, through the thick smoke and up to my room.

Why me? I thought. "There is nothing that could make this day any worse for me. Nothing," I shouted at my ceiling, but all the hollering in the world didn't change one fact: my mother had shown the entire neighborhood and those who serve the city how ridiculous she was.

I couldn't stay in my room. Because the kitchen is right below me, everything smelled like smoke. I opened the three windows on the east wall and the French doors that lead onto the small balcony I sometimes read on in the early mornings, and hoped for a breeze.

I was lucky. The evening winds came down out of Hobblecreek Canyon and blew through my room, cleansing the air, making the curtains dance and billow. But the wind couldn't take away a bit of my hard heart. So when Mom called up the stairs that we'd be eating at Mi Ranchito in Orem, I almost didn't go.

When Daddy insisted I come with them, and said Mary could come too, I agreed. So we wouldn't be eating home-cooked food. At least I could enjoy an evening with my best friend. Maybe we could sit at a separate table from my parents. Maybe I wouldn't have to look at my mother at all. Ever again.

That didn't quite work out. We hadn't been seated in the restaurant, munching chips with fresh salsa, even fifteen minutes when Mom tapped her water glass with a table knife.

"May I have your attention?" The way she said it, looking around the restaurant like maybe everyone in the world wanted to hear what she said, I could tell at least *she* thought she had important news.

Dad, Mary and I all looked at her. I was still angry.

"I've got wonderful news," Mom said. "Wonderful for all of us. Danny. Laura." Mom grinned like she did on those old magazine covers. "Mary, even you should be happy about this." Mom clasped her hands in front of her, still holding the knife. Lucky for her she didn't put out an eye.

"I just want you all to know"—Mom paused

like she expected a drumroll—"that I'm six months pregnant. We're going to have a baby."

things to change about MY MOTHER!!!!!!!

9. ***burning down the house***
10. ***Aaaaaaaaaaaaaaah!***

IT!!! . . .

I had thought nothing could be worse than my mother almost burning down the house. Watching my father try to free himself from the car had been pretty bad too. Seeing them in the restaurant dancing some made-up I-don't-know-what dance while a guitar player sang and grinned, that was awful. But none of those things was the worst.

I don't remember what I ate for dinner that evening. Maybe it was beef tacos. Maybe it was chicken enchiladas. Maybe it was my own plate. I was so horrified by Mom's announcement that all I could do was look at the ground. That was after I shouted, "What? You've been doing . . . you've been having . . . but you're so old." I glanced around, looking at the people who were staring at us.

"Not so loud, honey," Dad said through a wide, wide smile.

"I'm not that old," Mom said. "For heaven's sake, Laurie, I'm thirty-eight."

I leaned across the table, clutching my napkin. Knowing she was pregnant made my face burn. Just last year in Science Health I had seen the pictures about how a baby gets to be a baby. I knew what they had been doing. All of Mi Ranchito knew. "Mother. Do you know how close to forty you are?" I whispered through clenched teeth.

"Oh, Laura," Mary said. "This is great."

"Greatnotgreat," I said. I faced my friend. "She's forty. Four. Tee."

Dad laughed a little. "Honey, two years away. Two." He held up two fingers. I had no idea what he meant.

"You two are too old . . ." I wanted to say "too old to be doing the deed," but I was embarrassed. Mom and Dad were probably too old to know what that even meant.

Every time I saw my mother's pink face, and my father grinning, and then Mary smiling, smiling, smiling, I felt appalled.

Didn't my best friend get it?

Didn't they?

My mother and father, the oldest people in my immediate family, had been doing it. It. The it that would get my ancient mother pregnant. I thought they were too old for . . . for . . . you know. I couldn't even bring myself to say the word. I could barely think the first letter. *S.* I thought people stopped having you-know-what when they were about twenty-nine.

Mary leaned toward me. "Now you know," she whispered when Dad and Mom were toasting each other with caffeine-free Coca-Colas.

"I know what?" It felt like a tortilla chip was caught in my throat. Maybe it was just embarrassment.

"You know why your mom nearly burned down the house."

"No, I don't." I glared at Mary, my eyebrows pushed together.

"Sure you do. She's pregnant." Mary lifted her hands at me like I might find an answer for my parents' craziness hidden between her fingers.

"Ha!" I said. The only thing I knew now was why my mother was getting heavier. She *should* be heavier.

I should have noticed Mom was getting heavier, especially in her tummy area. The fact was, though, she wasn't that much bigger. I mean, her face looked a little puffy, but it was hard to notice. Mom didn't look a thing like Mariah Barry when *she* got pregnant. That girl porked right up, and it was her first baby. I only know that because she came to our house to talk to Mom about exercising and she said those very words. She said, "I've porked right up."

On the way home that night I tried to ignore my mother and father and best friend as they sang baby songs. *Baby* songs. I guess there were things to be thankful for. Dad wanted to stop at a music store so he could buy a guitar.

"I'm sure I could teach myself a song on the way to Mapleton," he said, pulling into Keith Jorgenson's. "It can't be that hard. Jimmey, you can drive us home."

"Okay, Danny," Mom said.

The store was closed, and even with all Dad's tapping on the window, the employees counting money at the cash register wouldn't open up for him.

"That's the last time I shop there," Dad said as he climbed into the car. "They could have let me in and they didn't."

The good thing was that the window I sat behind in the car was tinted. I was pretty sure no one in the store could see me.

In my room that night, after we dropped Mary off at home, I had a good long chance to think.

"I guess I wasn't expecting Mom to get pregnant." I said this to no one when I went out onto the balcony. It was a clear night, and the sky glittered with stars. The moon had yet to peek over the mountains, so it was pretty dark out. Only a hint of smoke smell remained in my room.

"I mean," I said, "she's miscarried all the other babies she's tried to have."

I had lost count, but I knew there were at least five miscarriages after I was born. Those Mom had spoken to me about. I remembered her talking to me a year or two before, when we still saw things the same way. She had been so sad.

"Laurie," she had said. "I really wanted a big family." We were in her studio, where she fashioned a little girl with fat cheeks, wearing only a diaper, from clay to be bronzed. Eventually this, too, would be added to her collection.

"I'm sorry, Mom." I breathed deep the smells of the orange clay and watched Mom's slender hands smooth the child's skin. I felt sort of sorry for my mother. A baby would have been a nice thing to have around the house.

But I felt a little guilty, too. I kind of liked being an only child. I had all Mom's attention. I worked clay with her. She taught me to draw. We went places together—did stuff. It was a nice life. For sure a baby would change all that.

I thought, as I sat on my little balcony, how lonely Mom must have been for another child. I mean, to try so many times. And now at such an old age. Good grief, she was nearly forty. If you ask me, the *S* word should be saved for the young. Not my age, but definitely not my mother's, either. For people on television.

I watched the moon rise and in the darkness

of the evening tried to follow the bats flying after mosquitoes. I thought of Mom and Dad, down the hall, doing It. I thought of the baby Mom carried. I thought of her almost burning our house down.

Yes, I had liked being the only child in the Stephan home. But I was tired of carrying this burden alone. If Mom and Dad had succeeded in having other babies, I would have been sharing this awful moment with a sibling. One that I am sure would have loved me and would pretty much have done everything I wanted him to do. Including hating the thought, like I did, of our mother being pregnant at the very old age of thirty-eight.

I pulled out my list.

things to change about MY MOTHER!!!!!!!

11. She's been doing It, very possibly here in the house.

(My face turned red when I wrote this.)

There wasn't much I could do about Mom's pregnant state. Pretty soon everyone at church and in the neighborhood would know that she and Dad were active. You'd think there would be a law about people as old as they are doing . . . well, you know.

Dad and the Area

It took me a week and a half before I could look at Mom and Dad without thinking how Mom ended up pregnant.

It didn't seem to bother anyone in the neighborhood *except* me. Mary told her parents and they were both excited, probably because there are six kids in their family and they are used to, well, you know. Then Mary told Christian when the three of us were playing a short game of basketball.

"Cool, Laura," Christian said. "A baby. Do you think it will be a boy or a girl?" He brushed his sandy blond hair out of his face.

"Yeah," I said, and then missed the next three shots. I usually win at that game too. Dad says I have a good eye and he's not sure where it came from, 'cause he's never played any athletic game in his life.

Later Quinn found out Mom was pregnant and said, "Tell her I said congrats."

My face turned red anytime anyone said anything about it, and the news spread like wildfire.

A couple of ladies from church came and visited Mom. They wanted to have a baby shower for her, they said. Our next-door neighbor Wendy Smith brought over dinner "just because." And to make matters worse, Mom seemed to glow.

I mean it. She got this cheery look on her face, and her cheeks always seemed to be pink. And then she tried to get chummy with me. She started asking me to do things with her. "Let's go to lunch, Laurie," or "Let me read this picture book to you, honey, to see if you think the new baby will like it," or "I'm going to try to learn how to knit, want to try too?"

It was sickening.

One afternoon Mom called me down from my room. I was reading *Dinah Forever,* by a lady named Claudia Mills. I was actually laughing at the things Dinah was going through. I kind of felt like her—pretty, smart, a new sibling. Well, almost for me.

"Laurie," Mom called. "I need you a second."

I put my Dinah book down and let out an

aggravated sigh. I stomped all the way to the living room, where Mom and Dad waited.

"What are you doing home from work?" I asked Dad. He usually isn't home until six or so. Unless there's a fire, of course. Anyway, he works in American Fork, and it always takes him a little while to get here.

"Two reasons," Dad said. He raised both pointer fingers. "First of all, we're going to see the ultrasound today." Dad reached over and patted Mom's belly. My face went red.

"Don't do that," I said. I looked toward the bay window. Outside the sun shone. A slight breeze moved the aspen trees, making the leaves shiver.

"Do what?" Dad asked.

"Don't pat Mom's . . . area."

Dad grinned. I have to admit that my father is very attractive. He may be a computer geek, but he looks great. His hair is thick and wavy and an almost blond color. His eyes are deep brown. He has a few freckles. *All* my girlfriends are always telling me how good looking he is. But then he does something like open his mouth and I am, most of the time, horrified.

"I'm patting the baby, Laura Anne," he said. "Your baby brother or baby sister is nestled in the protective *area*"—he emphasized the word *area*—"of the womb, or uterus. He or she is floating in amniotic fluid and appreciates it when I touch here. I believe the baby knows I am waiting just—"

"Dad," I said. I didn't want to hear any more of that crap. And I didn't want to see him patting anything of Mom's, either. I was just getting over the *s-e-x* part of things. "What did you all call me down here for?"

"We want you to come with us, Laurie," Mom said. "And we want to talk to you about throwing a party."

"What?"

Mom smiled at me. Dad put an arm around her shoulder and then he smiled too. I took a step backward.

"We've felt you needed something to cheer you up." Mom glanced at Dad. "We were thinking you could have your first boy-girl party. Here, at the house." Mom stretched her hands out wide, like maybe she was offering me the living room.

A party?

Dad stood up and pulled Mom to her feet. "We have to go. Wanna come? We can make plans on the way to the hospital."

A boy-girl party?

"Go get your shoes on," Mom said.

"Okay," I said. A boy-girl party! That could be fun. For a moment I saw myself inviting Quinn over. And maybe us dancing a slow dance together. I hurried up the stairs, grinning. Happy, for what seemed the first time in all my life.

things to change about MY MOTHER!!!!!!!

12. Mom allowing Dad to pat her area
13. It
14. IT
15. IT!!!

At the hospital the doctor uncovered Mom's ball of a belly. He squirted jelly stuff on her stomach and started rubbing what looked like a microphone all over the *area*.

I don't know what I expected. Maybe to see a picture of a baby as clear as any on TV. That's not what happened. There was a faint white outline of things that made no sense.

"There's the heart," the doctor said. "Looks healthy. Four chambers. Blood flow is great. Let's keep going. Spine is fine."

My eyes started adjusting.

Mom was bawling and Dad kept saying, "There, there," but I could hear tears in his voice, too.

"Oh, here we go," the doctor said. "It's a girl."

A girl? How could he see anything on that screen?

"A girl," Dad said, and his voice cracked right

in two, he was so happy. "I always wanted all girls."

"Can you show me her face?" Mom asked.

"Sure." The picture seemed to spin and then slow down. "Look at that," the doctor said. "She's sucking her thumb." He used an arrow to point things out.

It was then that I saw it. I saw the whole picture. I saw my sister sucking her thumb. She was still all funky looking, just a pale outline in a bluish black sea, but I could see her little hand up at her mouth. And even though I wasn't going to say a thing about it to my mom or dad, it was at that very moment that I fell in love with her, and I couldn't wait for her to be born.

My Party

"Now, of course you'll invite Christian, right, honey?" Mom asked. She sat at her desk in her office, a pad of paper in hand. We were making a list. No, *she* was making a list.

"Yes, Mom." I didn't want to look at her. I was angry. This was, after all, supposed to be my party. A party that I wanted to plan with Mary. How could I with Mom's nose stuck right in my business?

"And that little boy whose parents just put in the tennis courts?"

"Yeah, I guess so. That's Kevin." But he definitely is not a little boy. In fact, he is tall and skinny and has huge feet, something I couldn't help noticing in math class.

"The Cummingses are such good people," Mom said. So now she was giving her stamp of approval, was she? Suddenly I wished all my friends were people my mother wouldn't nod in acceptance over. Too bad at thirteen Kevin couldn't grow a long beard. That would make my mom hesitate before inviting him to my first boy-girl party.

I squinted and took in a deep breath. Beard for Kevin. Dreadlocks for Mary. Tattoo for Christian. Who else did Mom want to invite?

"Well, honey. Do you have any ideas?"

"You're doing fine," I said. And she was, too. But *I* wanted to do it.

"How about six and six?"

"Six and six what?"

"Boys and girls."

"Yeah, whatever." I looked around Mom's office, pretending this was okay. Her statues were everywhere, decorating shelves, standing in corners, near the edge of her desk. Mom was a wonderful sculptor. That's what Gary Price had said. He's a really famous guy. He'd called Mom "up-and-coming" and said he thought she had a lot of natural talent.

I like Mom's stuff too, but today it was getting on my nerves. It was . . . I don't know, too goody-goody. I mean, everything in the room had something to do with family: a man and a woman near an empty cradle, a pregnant woman with a sweater draped over her shoulders, a butterfly sitting on a flower with a little girl kneeling nearby.

Everything matched what Mom felt was important. *Especially* the statue she was working on now.

You know what sculpture you should work on instead, Mom? I thought. *The one of the mother making the party list for her daughter.* I wrinkled my forehead and looked down at my nails, which Mary's sister Karen had painted and even put decals on.

"Laura," Mom said. "Laura, what is the matter with you? I am trying to make this easier for you. A girl's first party—"

"Mom," I said, and the voice I used was not nice at all, but I couldn't stop it. "Mom, this is your party. Yours! You are inviting who you think I should have over here."

Mom's mouth dropped open a bit and her face looked a little like I'd just punched her in the gut. "I . . ."

"I thought this was going to be *my* party. I thought . . . what I thought was that *I'd* be able to work it out with Mary, that she and *I* could come up with people. But just like everything else in my life, you have taken over." This part wasn't the truth, and I was a little surprised when my mouth said it. But I didn't stop. In fact, I jumped to my feet and as I ran from Mom's office I shouted, "Just call me when you've taken care of the guest list."

I ran out the front door, slamming it behind

me. Taking the stairs two at a time, I started for Mary's house, not even looking back when Mom called my name.

"Let her do the party," I said as I ran. "Let her choose who she wants to come." I could see my list in my head. This had to be added to it.

things to change about MY MOTHER!!!!!!!
16. Mom running MY party

I ran the two blocks to my best friend's house, only to get there in time to see her leaving with her family.

"I'll be back in a couple of hours, Laura," Mary called out her rolled-down window. "We're going to the mall." For a moment I thought I might run after her. I didn't. Instead, I waved to her until their gray van was gone.

And then I thought I was going to start crying. Standing there near my best friend's house, I felt tears well up in my eyes, tears that seemed hotter than the summer air. "Come back," I said.

A door slammed over at the Sumsions' house and Quinn walked outside. His hair was wet and smoothed down. My stomach lurched when I saw him. "You are the cutest guy I've ever seen in all my life," I said, my voice lower than a whisper.

"Hey, Laura," he called. He lifted his hand in a partial wave and smiled.

I sucked air in through my teeth and, without

meaning to, made a hissing noise. "Hi, Quinn." My tears dried right up.

"Coming to play ball?"

Was he asking me? I looked around. I was alone.

I shrugged and walked toward him, passing the houses that separated us. "I'm planning a party," I said. "My first boy-girl party."

"Is that right?" Quinn looked over his shoulder, back toward the door.

"Yeah," I said. "Wanna come?" What? What had my mouth just done? I was close enough that I could see his eyes get bigger.

"To your party?" Quinn asked, and his voice was full of surprise. "You're inviting me to your party?"

My face seemed to freeze up. I gave a sort of nod.

Right at that moment the side door of Quinn's house opened and out walked Christian and the most beautiful girl this side of my mother. She had dark hair that fell to her waist, and eyes so blue that even from where I stood I could see them. Her makeup was perfect, her body was perfect, even her nails were perfect. I hated her right away. If I was lucky, she'd have a voice like Mickey Mouse's.

"Quinn," she said. Her voice was deep and smooth. "You ready to go?"

"Wait, Rebecca," Quinn said. "Laura here has invited . . ."

"Don't," I said, my voice soft. The sun seemed hotter than usual. It felt like it shone only on me, like I was in a spotlight.

". . . me to her first boy-girl party. Are you jealous?"

For one moment I had been so happy to see Quinn that I didn't think anything could destroy it. I was, of course, wrong. This girl was with him. They were like perfect bookends or bronzes my mother might sculpt. And was Quinn making fun of me? Hot sun. Hot. Hot. Hot.

"A party?" Rebecca leaned toward me and I waited for biting words. But that didn't happen. She smiled. Quinn smiled too. "I love parties. And I remember my first one, too. It was so much fun."

Christian moved over near me and I tried not to look at him. I was so embarrassed even my lips felt cooked.

"I just thought—" I started, but Quinn cut me off.

"Hey," he said. He scooped Rebecca up in his arms. "I don't remember being invited to that."

She tilted her head and said, "I left you out on purpose, Quinn."

He pretended a pout, then turned to me.

"Thanks for the invite, Laura, but I don't think

we can make it. Ask Christian in my place. And the two of you, no kissing. You know Mom's rule." With that he planted a smacky kiss on Rebecca's lips. "Let's get going," he said.

And they did.

I stood in the burning sun next to Christian without moving until he said, "Um, Laura. A party? Really?" He kicked at the sidewalk, then went over and got the basketball.

I was too embarrassed to look at him, so instead I stared at the hoop that was there at the edge of the driveway. "Yeah," I said.

I heard the ball bounce three times.

Strike me dead, I thought. *God, strike me dead right now.*

We were silent a moment.

"Let's play some," Christian said.

"Sure."

Christian tossed me the ball, but for a moment I wasn't quite sure what to do.

"Hey. Did you just want Quinn, or am I invited too?" Christian asked. A bird twittered in a pine.

A bit of relief washed over me. "Yeah, I want you to be there," I said. I looked over his shoulder 'cause I couldn't quite look him in the eyes. "Yeah, sure."

And at that moment I really, *really* meant it.

The Man She Married

A note waited for me on my bed when I came home. It was short and simple.

Laura—

I'm so sorry. I didn't mean to take over your life. Please let me know what day you want the party.

Love,

Mom

I stood still, holding the slip of paper like it was made of gold. I read it five times to make sure it said what I thought it said. "Please let me know what day you want the party." It didn't say, "Who are you inviting?" or "What is the list of food?" or anything like that. She was letting me be in charge. Me. *I was the boss of my party.*

My hands started trembling and I ran to the phone. Mary could help me plan it and . . . I wanted to let out a shout of excitement. Instead I called my best friend and we spent the next two hours making plans.

Four days later I waited at the door, so nervous I thought I was going to puke. Mary and I had decorated the game room, and now the lights were low and dance music filled the air. Our Ping-Pong table was covered with all different kinds of food, drinks and desserts.

Mary had been with me all morning, and now she peeked from Mom's office window with me, watching the driveway for people to show up. The lights were out in here. I mean, I didn't want people to see us looking so eager. That would be embarrassing.

Christian was the first to arrive. He and Spencer Miller.

"I love Spencer," Mary said, and she squeezed my hand so hard it hurt.

Seeing Christian embarrassed me a little. I mean, I had made a fool of myself in front of him with his brother. The thought of Quinn with Rebecca made my heart ache. The thought of Christian trying to rescue me made my face warm. What in the world was the matter with me? All I ever did was feel embarrassed or angry or frustrated. But there was no time to think about that now.

The bell rang, and Mary and I took our time walking the few feet to open the front door.

"Hey, you guys," I said. "We're down in the game room. Mary will show you the way." I felt a little like a hostess for something really important. And I guess I was, too. My first boy-girl party.

Mary, Christian and Spencer had barely left the room when Mom and Dad came in.

"Laura," Mom said. She held her hands up like a shield, like maybe I was going to say something and she needed to stop me in advance. "I'm not trying to intrude."

"What?" I rolled my eyes. I wasn't angry with her, not like I had been; I was too excited about the party for that. But I didn't want her to think I wanted her to hang around. No, things were good now, with Mom leaving me alone. I liked it this way and I wanted to keep it this way.

Mom saw my face, saw that I was unhappy with her, and avoided my eyes.

"I was just thinking," she said. "I was just thinking that your dad and I would stay up here and usher people down for you. Then you could make sure things are going well with the party."

My heart softened a half-inch. But I didn't let it show. Instead I paused, pretended to think about her suggestion and then said, "Oh, all right." I let out a sigh and started off to the game room, glad to be where the party would happen.

The thing is, even after everyone got there, the party didn't really get going. The guys kind of stood on one side of the room, and we girls stood on the other. I could hear Christian telling all the guys about Quinn and basketball. In slow motion I worked my way to that side of the room. Would he tell all these guys about how I had asked his twenty-something-year-old brother to come to my twelve-year-old party?

"Hey, Laura," Christian said.

"Oops," I said. I hurried back to my side of the room. I would not make a good detective, I decided as I got close to Mary.

After a little bit I suggested we eat, and for a moment the twelve of us mingled, at least in the food line. Then back to our separate sides of the room again.

"Now what?" I asked Mary.

She stood close to me, watching the guys, her shoulder touching mine. "We could dance, Laura," she said in a loud voice. She looked straight at Spencer, who was drinking punch, when she said this.

"Dance?" I said.

And then Dad showed up.

"Halftime entertainment," he said, coming into the room in the ugliest clothes I have ever seen in my life. A pair of blue jeans with silver tacking going down the sides and a shiny purple shirt, both a little too small. I knew they were things he had been saving since he dated Mom, I could tell by looking at them. These were '80s clothes and I bet they scared everyone in the room. I know they scared me.

Dad had a CD in his hand, and as he came in he said, "We kind of noticed that things weren't cooking in here. . . ."

Cooking?

"So, Laura, if we have your permission, your mom and I thought we'd do a few dance steps from our day and age."

I shook my head. "No, Dad," I said.

Everyone looked at me. Was I as wide-eyed as my friends were? "Better not," I said.

There was a bit of an awkward silence, and then Christian said, "Sure, Mr. Stephan. We'd love to see you two dance."

Dad didn't wait a second longer. Instead he threw back his head and hollered out, "No parking on the dance floor, baby!"

What? Discomfort washed over me like a hot liquid.

Mom came in then, dressed in clothes I think she wore when she was pregnant with me.

"Uh, wait," I managed to say. I lifted a hand.

Mom waved at me, then said, "Party on, Wayne," copying an old movie she and Dad watch all the time.

I felt the blood in my face drain down to my toes. Did I have a sudden fever? Some horrible disease that caused me to feel like this? First a wave of fire, then ice, washed over me. Fire. Ice. Fire. Ice. For a moment I thought I might faint. Christian came close, touching me with his arm.

Mary laughed and started clapping as Dad walked over to the stereo and slipped in his special music.

Without meaning to, I grabbed Christian's shirtsleeve.

"This is going to be great," he said.

Please, God, I prayed. *Please don't let this be happening.*

But it was. Michael Jackson's voice boomed out of the stereo so loud I bet it frightened the baby Mom was carrying.

Dad grabbed Mom by one hand and slung her to the other side of the room. Zach Terry started clapping out the beat of the music, and pretty soon everyone but me had joined him. My eyeballs felt like only blood vessels held them in my head. I probably looked like something gross from *The X-Files.*

I could barely look at Mom and Dad. Sure, they were good dancers . . . for the olden days. But why did they have to do it now? Why at my party?

Mom and Dad spun this way and that, weaving between each other's arms, wiggling so that I thought I might die. At least I wished it.

"Wanna try?" Christian asked.

"You mean me? Do that?" I pointed at my parents.

"Why not?" Christian gave a shrug.

I had no time to answer.

"Dance lessons," Dad called out, and he grabbed Maggie Lauritzen by the hands and started dancing with her. Mom took Isaac Allred and whispered something to him. He grinned and started moving his feet. Dance lessons? Eek.

"Dirty dog," Mom shouted, and then she was moving in a way that made the boys guffaw with laughter and follow her around the room, copying her. Everyone was dancing now, everyone but me. Mary danced with Spencer, Kevin danced with Shauna, Lance danced with Jacqui. People were laughing and clapping and, well, really having fun.

"Come on," Christian said. "Come on, Laura." He grabbed me and we nearly slipped apart, my hands were so sweaty.

"Sorry," I whispered, wiping my hands on my jeans.

Christian just smiled.

It's okay, I told myself. *This is okay.* I said a silent prayer that things would continue like this, and that Mom and Dad wouldn't have to stay with us for the party to keep being fun. I unclenched my fists and started relaxing. I even started enjoying myself.

"The swing," Mom called out. She and Dad did steps from that, whizzing around the room. Mom's long blond hair flew out behind her.

"The hustle," Dad yelled.

"You're reaching," Mom said, and I wasn't sure what she meant, but Dad just laughed. Then the two of them started with simple steps that everyone tried to follow, moving fast to stay with Michael Jackson's rhythm. Christian and I tried too, but he didn't let go of my hand until Mary said, "I know a line step. It's easy."

"Good deal," Dad said, and he and Mom danced back to let Mary show the way. We all copied her, and I have to admit, it was fun. *I* was having fun, something I didn't think possible with my parents around.

Mom and Dad danced a minute more, then, taking each other's hands, started to leave the room.

Thank you, I said in my head. The thank-you was to them for getting things going and to God for getting my parents to leave.

"Hey," said Christian. "Show us one more eighties thing." His arm almost cradled my back, like he might be holding on to me.

"No," said Mom. "We're old." For some reason she patted her tummy.

"Come on," said Derek. "Do some break dancing for us. Can you do that?"

I saw Dad hesitate, start toward us, then hesitate again. "Well," he said, drawing the word out, "I used to be a pretty good breaker." He stopped one more time.

"Show us," Shauna said. "Show us."

"Yeah," Christian said.

Mom gave Dad a slight push forward.

I mouthed the word "No," but Dad didn't see me.

"Oh, all right," Dad said, and he threw his hands up in the air like we were making him do something he didn't really want to do, but I could tell by the look on his face that he was getting a kick out of showing off for my friends.

"It's been a lot of years," he said. "Honey, put on 'Beat It.' "

Mom forwarded the CD to the song, and after a brief silence the sound of electric guitars filled the air around us. Dad, in his socks, went up onto his tippy-toes, stood there a moment, wobbling, then with the rhythm of the song began to move in ways I have never seen him move. I watched with only one eye, afraid to give him my full attention. And he did pretty good.

He twirled around on his heel, tipped a fake hat and swung his hips.

"Moonwalk," Mom called out, and Dad slid

backward on the wooden floor in an almost magical way. Everybody clapped, Mom loudest of all.

"Spider crawl," Mom called again, and Dad held his hands behind his legs and moved like a huge, slightly overweight spider might.

"Fleet-flights," Mom shouted.

Dad fell to the floor and started spinning on his back. The next thing I knew, he was on his shoulders, then up on his head, his arms and legs flying through the air like a slow propeller. He was like that all of eight seconds, his face turning red, then his neck teetered a little and with a grunt he fell to his shoulder. His legs went over the top of his head like he had started a backward roll and gotten caught in the middle.

"Laura," Mom shouted, and she waved her hand up and down like she was hailing a taxi. I ran and turned off the music. The circle of my friends moved closer to my father, whose rear end stuck up in the air like a blue-jean island.

Mary grabbed my arm, and Maggie leaned close to me and whispered, "Oh no." Jacqui and Lance, holding hands, seemed frozen. Christian had an almost-smile on his face.

Mom went down on her knees. "Danny? Danny? Are you okay?"

"No," Dad said. It was more like a grunt than a word.

My face lost all color, then turned beet red in less than a second. I couldn't breathe for embarrassment. My nose, it seemed, had stopped working.

"Can you move your legs?" Mom took hold of one of Dad's feet.

"Don't do it," Dad said, his voice all squishy sounding. "I heard something snap in my neck. If you move my legs, I may be paralyzed for life."

I was sure at that moment that there was no God. Unless, of course, He likes jokes.

The most incredible thing about the whole evening was that Dad stayed in that position until the paramedics arrived.

things to change about MY MOTHER!!!!!!!

17. dancing pregnant

18. dancing at all

19. the man she married

Up in my room, with everyone gone, including the ambulance, I realized that there was going to be only one person I could depend on: my unborn baby sister.

Protecting the Guilty: My Father

I was right in the middle of a dream where Michael Jackson was screaming "Beat Him" at the top of his lungs, when a tapping woke me.

For a moment I felt all right. I mean, the sun was streaming through my window, everything seemed cozy, my room looked the perfect shade of yellow.

Then I remembered and it seemed even my cheerful room turned black.

Last night. Oh, the horrors of last night. Lying in bed, I broke out in a sweat. I squeezed my eyes shut again, slapping my hand to my forehead. Nothing would take away the sick, sinking feeling in my heart and stomach. Not even seeing Quinn. Oh, thank goodness he hadn't come.

The tapping sounded again, like a distant woodpecker. It was Mom. She pushed open the door a bit and peeked in at me. "Laurie girl, you asleep?"

My mother's voice brought back a flood of memories that I wished would wash me to a deserted island.

The ambulance, the men working to lower Dad flat on his back. One of the EMTs laughing behind his hand. Mom jumping into the ambulance and shouting out, "No, really, you all have a great time. Don't let this spoil anything."

Yeah, right. Was I going to throw up now?

"Daddy's sleeping," Mom told me, and plopped herself on my bed.

"Is his neck broken?" I asked—already knowing the answer.

Mom let out a little sigh. "No, thank goodness, it's not. In fact, he's—"

"Fine," I finished for her.

"No," Mom said, her voice a little bristly. "He's not fine. His neck *was* injured."

"Does he have a cast? A full-body cast? That's what I think he would need after his little"—I rolled toward the wall, turning my back on Mom—"his little performance."

Mom leaned over me, petting my hair and trying to make me look at her. Her belly was in the small of my back.

"I've never been so embarrassed in my life," I said. My eyes watered from the memory of Dad and his blue-jeaned bottom. It was true. I mean, out of everything that seemed to be happening—all at once, if you ask me—this had to be the worst of all. "If you both had just stayed upstairs where you belonged . . ." A whimper caught me at the end of my sentence, making the word *belonged* a squeak.

Mom's voice was apologetic. "Honey, we made a mistake. We thought . . . we thought because the party was going a little slow . . ."

All in one motion I rolled into a sitting position and glared at Mom.

"Look," I said. "Things were slow. I know that. But they were *my* kind of slow. It was *my* problem. If you could just back off a little. Let me breathe. But you won't." Tears threatened to spill. I held my eyes wide open so they would not.

Mom got to her feet. "We're going to Village Inn for breakfast," she said after a little pause. "If you want to go, get dressed."

It wasn't long after that that I heard Mom crying. Just soft sobs that came from her room. I tiptoed down the hall toward her, still dressed in my nightclothes, and listened at the door.

"It's just an age," I heard my dad say. "Remember, you told me you went through that very thing."

"But, Danny, she used to be my best friend. I was never my mother's best friend."

A tiny bit of sadness caught me in the throat. It was true. Mom and I had been close.

"I'm going to talk to her," Dad said. He sounded mad.

"Now, wait."

"No, I'm not waiting." Dad's voice got closer. I backed away from their door, ready to run. "She doesn't have to like us, but she does have to be kind to us."

Mom let out a big sob. "But I *want* her to like me."

Dad's voice got smaller again. "Oh, baby," he said, and I knew he was going to cuddle my mother.

"Good," I said in a low voice. "Good that she and I *aren't* friends." I marched down to my room, feeling a mixture of emotions. One was relief that Mom and I weren't friends anymore. The other was sorrow. I pushed the sorrow away by looking at my list. There! No guilt at all! None required! Getting out a purple gel pen, I wrote.

things to change about MY MOTHER!!!!!!!
20. her protecting the guilty
(I mean DAD)

As far as I was concerned, they owed me breakfast. No, they owed me an apology. No—they owed me sanctuary.

I looked at myself in the mirror that hung over the oak dresser in my room and changed clothes. What a sad person I was. Everything on my face seemed to droop.

"Sanctuary," I said to my reflection. My life was worse than poor Quasimodo's. "Sanctuary." At least I thought it was. I'd tried to read *The Hunchback of Notre Dame*, but it was, well, too much for me. I had seen the Disney movie, though. Frollo had never, not once, done any kind of dancing in front of Quasimodo's friends. So he kept him in a bell tower. So what? At the end of the movie everything turned out perfect. And how would my life be? Hmmm? There was no answer. Just an embarrassing father led by an embarrassing mother. How fair was that?

"Sanctuary." This time I whispered the word. Then, "My life . . . sucks."

Oh, I looked sad. So, so sad.

I leaned into the mirror and watched as my eyes filled with tears. The tears leaked onto my lashes and sat there a moment, trembling. "Sanctuary." I said this as a tear fell, dripping onto my dresser top.

"Laura?" Dad's voice startled me, making two more tears fall from my eyes. "We're leaving in ten minutes."

"Coming," I whispered. I headed to the living room, hunched over a little and limping, dressed in shorts and a T-shirt. Today promised to be a hot one. June in Utah can be a scorcher, though I have to admit August is the worst time for heat. September was when the baby would come.

On the sofa I relived last night. In my mind I heard Spencer say, "That was the oddest position for someone to be in." I had heard a wheezy sound like someone had pneumonia and was trying to draw a beep breath. I had looked toward the sound and seen it was Mary. *Mary* starting to laugh.

My best friend, I had thought. My eyes felt buggy as I looked at each person in the room.

Her laughter, though, set it all off. Pretty soon everyone was laughing their head off. Except me. Sure, if it had been one of *their* fathers who had tried to do some break dancing and had gotten stuck with his butt in the air, *that* would have been a different story. *That* would have been funny.

But no one's father would have tried it, I thought now, sitting on the sofa, staring out the window at the very sunny morning. No one's father would have thought that after fifteen years he could still be a champion break-dancer.

No one's father would have been wearing clothes from another era. Only my dad, only my mom, would do those things.

"It's funny," Shauna had said. She had wiped tears from her eyes. Not Quasimodo tears, happy tears.

"I hope he's okay," Jacqui had said, and Lance had said, "I hope the breaking didn't really break him." Again my friends shrieked.

I squeezed my eyes shut at the memory, of people wandering away, going home, still laughing. Of Christian turning around to say goodbye, and instead just waving, with laughter seeming to bubble from him.

"Laura?" Dad's voice pulled me out of last night.

"Yeah?" I looked at him. There he stood in his blue jeans—ones that fit, thank goodness—and a shirt that said, ORLANDO IS WHERE IT'S AT!

His neck was in a brace—just like a geek, if you ask me. In black marker he had written the words "BEAT IT" BEAT ME UP. I looked away.

"Now, Laura, honey," he said. "You know I did not mean to injure myself."

"Sure you didn't," I whispered. I didn't want him to hear me, but I couldn't stand to be silent, either.

"For a while there I really thought my neck was broken."

"Uh-huh."

Dad's words brought the image of his larger-than-life butt sticking up in the air. The memory caused a genuine pain to hit me right in the gut. I mean, it actually hurt. Probably as bad as a knife would. Or pulling the ropes of a huge bell in a tower. *Sanctuary*, I thought.

"I couldn't know I . . ." Dad paused. Was he embarrassed too? Well, he sure as heck should be!

"I couldn't know that it was just a mild sprain. I did hear that snap. I thought it was broken."

Dad walked over and sat on the sofa. He slipped his arm around my shoulders, wincing a little when he turned to look at me.

"Honey," Dad said, and his voice was really low. "You gotta treat your mom better. You have to be nice to her. Can't you treat her like you used to?"

I took a deep breath. "Dad, things have changed between Mom and me," I said. "Things have just changed." And as soon as I said it, I knew it was true.

Elmo

Once those words were out, that things had changed, the way I looked at life seemed to change too.

All of a sudden I would feel sad about something. A chord of music I heard on the radio or a commercial I saw on TV would get me in the gut. Tears would well up in my eyes. I couldn't re-watch the Hunchback movie. Somehow this seemed connected to Mom and me. The sadness, I mean.

At night, at times, I would wake up and hear Mom walking around downstairs, searching for something in the fridge maybe, or just because she was uncomfortable, and my heart would feel all stretched out from loneliness. Sure, Mary was a wonderful best friend. But Mom. She had been a *different* kind of best friend.

"Why did you have to change?" I would whisper. Then my eyes would fill with hot tears, and my throat would choke me, so that I'd have to sit up to catch my breath.

One late night I decided I wanted a bit of that back—our friendship. *If* Mom was willing to stop doing stupid things, *I* was willing to be her friend again. I went to sleep feeling everything would be okay, and the next day when she asked me to run with her to the store for food, I said yes.

"Go wait for me in the car," Mom said. She handed me the keys. "You can start it if you want."

I smiled at my mother, trying not to notice how tired she looked.

She was pretty pregnant, just over seven months, her tummy really sticking out. And her bosoms had gotten huge. It seemed like all at once she—what had Dad called it? Blossomed? Yeah, that was what he had said. "Your mother has blossomed, Laura."

But *blossomed* seemed the wrong word to me. To tell you the truth, she looked kind of wilted, like she needed a good watering or something. She'd tied her hair up in a halfhearted ponytail and she wore no makeup. Her face was puffy, her eyes were puffy, her ankles were puffy. If you ask me, she was a puffball.

I noticed her ankles right off because of the Elmo slippers she had on. I stared at her feet.

"I'll turn on the radio," I said, staring, "to that station you like while you change into your shoes."

"I'll be there in a second," she said. "Let me grab my wallet and see if I can find that list."

"I think your brown shoes will look good with your outfit." Really this was a lie. I couldn't quite remember what Mom had on. The Elmo slippers seemed to have hypnotized me and at the same time fogged my memory.

Mom padded out of the room and my trance was broken. I started to the car, calling out behind me, "Or your moccasins. They'd look great."

The car was in the garage, and I had to go through Mom's studio to get there.

When Mom and Dad were having this place built, right after they were married, Mom didn't know she was going to be a good sculptor, but she was hoping. Not only did she and Dad have six bedrooms built in this house (with room to grow in the basement) for babies they would someday have, but she also had a studio designed for herself.

This room is huge and full of windows, on both the west and east walls, so she gets a lot of light in here. One wall is loaded with cabinets and shelves. These hold all her different art supplies. The other wall she has filled with pictures. Pictures of Dad and me. Pictures of the three of us together. Pictures, I realized, that were of our lives before Mom changed.

I was on my way to look through them when I saw Mom's latest piece of sculpture. It was on a stand, half born it seemed. A baby. A new baby.

My breath caught as I looked at this thing so tiny and curled up and lifelike. The face wasn't finished yet, but the hands were perfect. One curled into a tiny fist. The other lay open, like maybe it expected a small gift. All at once, I wanted my little sister here with us, safe and sound.

Heavenly Father, I thought. *It's time for me to have some company.*

The thick smell of clay, kind of an oily smell, filled Mom's studio. A shadow passed on the floor and I realized Mom was going to the garage from the outside.

I ran through her studio out into the garage and hopped into the car. I hit the door opener on the visor and behind me the big white door started rolling up. Mom got to the car before I could even start the engine.

"Hey, babe," she said, climbing up onto the seat. She gave a grunt and helped pull herself in with the steering wheel.

Elmo stared at me from the gas pedal, and then his twin appeared near the brake.

"Mom," I said. "Mo-om." I pointed.

"What, Laurie girl?" Then she looked to her

feet. "Oh, that. Honey, you gave me these for Christmas last year. Aren't they great?" Mom raised her eyebrows like I should believe what she said.

I ignored her gift comment. "Mom."

"You know how I love Elmo."

"Mom." A bit of sadness crept into my heart and traveled out along my skin. She didn't care enough about me to change her shoes.

Mom started the car.

"Laurie," she said, backing out of the garage and making a sweeping turn in the driveway. "Laurie, my feet are so swollen I can't put on any shoes at all. None. Well, maybe your dad's would work."

She braked the car hard enough that I bounced in the seat a little. "Should I go get some of his? His tennis shoes?"

I looked at Mom's swollen face, then out the window. "Maybe," I said after a moment. "We are going to the store. In public."

Mom put the car in park, then threw the Elmos into the backseat. "Hold on one second. You can get my station for me. I'll see what I can do."

I waited till Mom was out of the car before I started fiddling with the radio. First, though, I watched her waddle to the door. I mean it too. She waddled. Did she have to do that?

When she came back to the car, she wore a

pair of Dad's ancient penny loafers. Elton John blasted from the radio, singing about freedom in Philadelphia.

"Honey," Mom said when she hoisted herself into the car. "Honey, I don't think this is any better. I'm afraid these won't stay on."

I looked at her feet. They were tanned, puffy and swimming, almost, in Dad's shoes.

"I'm gonna have to go Elmo," she said.

I should have known that we would see everyone I knew from school, a few people from church and some people from the neighborhood at the local grocery store. It was Meet Elmo at Allen's Day, it seemed. Embarrassing.

And we were in the checkout line when I heard Quinn Sumsion call, "Hey, Mrs. Stephan. I got me some Oscar the Grouch slippers at home."

things to change about MY MOTHER!!!!!!!

21. Elmo

Bosoms and Bellies

A few days later Mom made an announcement at the table. Maggie Lauritzen was over for the night and so was Mary. The three of us had planned an evening of watching old movies down in the basement theater, staying up all night talking and eating junk food. We had come to the dinner table dressed in pajamas.

The sun still sat high in the sky. Dad had brought home Thai food for dinner. The house was cool and smelled like roses.

Mom looked at everyone after we had said a blessing. "I have an announcement." I was glad she didn't tap her water glass like she had in the Mexican restaurant. "Something happened to me today."

"What now?" I asked. "Twins?"

"Laura," Mary said. She slapped at my hand. Already she smiled at my mother.

"No, Laurie," Mom said. "You are so funny. Something happened today. It was a good thing."

We all looked at her. I prayed that this had nothing to do with disco dancing . . . or whatever that was that had frozen my father in the butt-up position.

"I got a call from the Rocky Mountain Fitness Center in Spanish Fork. The manager noticed when I was working out"—Mom lifted both hands high into the air, like maybe she hefted weights herself, even though really she just held a bottle of soy sauce—"that I'm going to have a baby. And guess what?"

"He noticed you're pregnant?" I said. "Hmm. That's a surprise."

Mom pretended not to hear me. Instead she talked to my friends and my father, who all leaned toward her. Maggie's short brown hair hung over her peanut-butter curry. Mary looked from Mom to me, then back to Mom again. Now she grinned.

"What, Jimmey?" Dad said. "What happened? Ignore the Oldest Child."

"They asked me to be in a television commercial. For their fitness center. To be aired everywhere in the West where they have a gym." Mom pursed her lips like she does when she's trying to hide a surprise from me.

"What?" I said. Only it wasn't really a *what* that came out. More of a *grock*.

"The Rocky Mountain Fitness Center," Mom said again. "Can you believe it?"

"You took a modeling job?" Dad asked.

"Yes!" Mom said.

"You're kidding," Mary said, and she swung her head in my direction and grinned even bigger. "Cool, Mrs. Stephan. The Rocky Mountain Fitness Center."

"Yeah," said Maggie. "That is *really* neat. My brother works out there."

"The Rocky Mountain Fitness Center. Hmmm. But you're . . . um . . . you're showing," I said. I gestured with my eyebrows at Mom's belly, which was hidden beneath the table.

"What?" Mom asked.

"I said, you're *showing*. It's *no-tice-able* that you are pregnant." A bit of sticky rice seemed to have gotten stuck right in the middle of my throat. I swallowed to make it go down, but it wouldn't budge. In fact, it felt like it was expanding. "I don't think you want people to notice that you are . . . um . . . in the family way."

Mom picked up a spring roll. She held on to it like it was a delicate cup filled with tea. "That's the exciting part of the commercial. It's for *pregnant* people."

From outside I heard our neighbor's dog start barking. Was he excited too?

"Tell us all about it," Dad said. He put his elbows on the table and rested his chin on his hands. He looked at Mom with dreamy eyes. She looked back at him with dreamy eyes. Maybe it was dreamy eyes that had begun this whole pregnant incident. I felt they should stop it right this second.

"Stop it," I said. "Right this second."

Now both my parents ignored me.

"Cool," said Maggie. She looked around the table like she knew something no one else did. "I know a TV star."

"A pregnant TV star," I said. The Thai food was starting to smell kind of greasy. "Your belly will show," I said to my mother.

"I know!" Mom smiled, then broke out into a huge grin. Her white teeth seemed to sparkle. Like maybe *we* were making a commercial at our dinner table: the beautiful, hugely pregnant woman with her husband, also happy, and three children—young adults, I mean—all beaming. Sort of. There was me. My mouth tried to beam, tried to look happy, but I knew I was failing. My lips had the sneer feel to them.

"Your . . ." I pointed my fork at her.

"What?" Mom asked.

"Your . . ."

"My . . ." Mom's voice was a prompt. Her hands helped, waving at me.

"Your. Bosoms."

Mom's head tilted a little to the left, then to the right. I felt my face turn pink.

Mary gave a sniff that I knew meant I had embarrassed her.

Maggie looked down at her plate.

"They. Are. Huge." I finished my sentence and gave a cough. Sticky rice flew out of my mouth and landed on the table near a vase of water that held three pink-and-yellow roses.

Mom bit her bottom lip like she was giving the word *bosoms* deep consideration.

"I do have two of them," she said.

Dad let out a bark of a laugh.

"I have heard of people with extra nipples, though," Mom said.

"Stop right there," I said. "Please don't embarrass me any further. Or my friends."

For sure, both Mary and Maggie looked embarrassed. The *N* word had definitely gotten to them.

"Your *breasts*," I said, emphasizing the word even though it caused Maggie to giggle, "will show. So will your belly."

"Bosoms and bellies," Dad said. "It sounds like a jelly or something."

"Mom. Stop Dad. He's grossing us all out. Are you two grossed out?" I looked at Mary and Maggie, but they both shook their head. "Yes you are," I said. "And I know you know it."

Finally Mom said, "Laurie, I promise to wear a bra."

"Or two," I said.

Late that night, once Mary and Maggie had both gone to sleep, I lay in my sleeping bag and stared at the ceiling. Through a large window I could see stars that seemed to wink at me, teasing almost.

"Don't be ridiculous," I said, keeping my voice low. "This has nothing to do with stars. It has everything to do with Mom."

I knew exactly what the problem was. Mom—pregnant—in front of the world, for everyone to see. She was huge now. Why would anyone want a pregnant lady advertising their gym? So what if she had a pretty face? "Come to the Rocky Mountain Fitness Center and you can look like me."

"Jeez." I sat up and wrapped my arms around my legs, then rested my chin on my knees.

Mary moved a little, then said, "Laura? Why are you up?"

"Just thinking," I said, "about Mom being in that commercial."

"Isn't that cool?" Mary asked, and her voice was all thoughtful sounding. In a moment I heard a slight snore and knew she was back asleep.

"Easy for you to say," I whispered. "Your mother is normal."

things to change about MY MOTHER!!!!!!!
(Where was that list?)

22. ***the two of us living in the same state—no, the same country***
23. ***bosoms and bellies***

If those people at the fitness center were thinking, they'd keep Mom covered from head to toe. An image of her in a towel that didn't quite cover her backside came to mind.

"Please don't let that happen," I prayed. "Don't let her be in only a towel. Even if it's a really, really big towel."

When I finally slept, I dreamed of Mom walking through a gym, dressed in a slick exercise outfit, not a bit pregnant.

Blowing Her Nose—Blowing My Cover

The next morning we slept late. I was awakened by Mom talking to . . . to . . . ? I could hear someone else and the voice was familiar, but I couldn't quite figure out who it was. I crawled out of my sleeping bag, quiet so I wouldn't wake anyone.

I made my way up the stairs like a kitten. Mom stood in the kitchen. I could hear her, plain as day, even though I couldn't see her. She was saying, "Are you sure you don't want any breakfast? Most times I don't start a fire when I'm cooking breakfast."

And then the other voice. "No thanks, Mrs. Stephan. Mom made oatmeal before I left."

Oatmeal? I thought. *Yucko.* I held on to the cherry-wood banister and dug my toes into the soft brown carpet that covers a lot of the basement floor.

"Oatmeal?" Mom said. "Well, it is very good for you. But . . . oatmeal." I could almost see Mom shivering. Just the thought of some foods makes Mom want to puke. I turned and began to tiptoe back down the stairs.

"Let's not talk about that, Christian," Mom said.

Christian? What was *he* doing here? I froze, my foot ready to take a step.

"Let's get back to talking about Laurie instead."

I spun toward their voices, my hair swirling out a little, I turned so hard. Talking about me? Could it be . . . oh, could it be that Quinn liked me now? Could something have changed? Was Rebecca out of the picture? I sank to the step, my hands clenched like I was ready for a long prayer.

Christian cleared his throat. "She'd kill me if she knew we were talking about her."

"Oh, no," Mom said. "She'd be pleased."

I could see the moss-colored marble floor and the very edge of the stainless-steel refrigerator, but that was all. I took another step up.

"I don't know. I've seen her pretty mad at you. If she can be that mad at her own mother, well, I think she could rip my head off and puke down my neck."

Mad? Mad at my own mother? Well, of course I had been a little upset. . . .

"Don't talk about puking, honey," Mom said. "It does something to my gag reflex."

"Sorry."

Christian was quiet a moment. I took the opportunity to move one step closer, hoping that the barfing comment hadn't made Mom ready to throw up in the kitchen sink. And what in the heck did Christian mean that I could rip his head off and puke like that, anyway? That was gross.

"She really is a nice girl," Mom said. I heard a tapping noise, like she was drumming the countertop.

"I know it," Christian said. "I've known it since we were six."

"That is so sweet!" Mom sounded a little choked-up.

Since we were six? What in the heck was that supposed to mean?

"I wouldn't even talk to you about this, but I know you know her and . . ."

"I do know her," Mom said. "Sometimes."

Sometimes? I leaned my head a little, pushing my left ear toward their conversation.

"Well, yeah," said Christian. "And see, I know she likes Quinn and . . ."

He knew I liked Quinn? How . . . I mean . . . what . . . I mean . . . why . . . I mean . . . it showed? I clutched at my pajama top with one hand and came half a swallow away from choking myself on my own spit.

"Well, every time I'm with her . . ." Christian stopped talking for a second. "Are you okay, Mrs. Stephan? Why are you crying? Did I say something wrong?"

I heard Mom give a sniff.

"No," she said, and her voice was all squeaky. "It's just that sometimes she's so unhappy with me that to hear you talk about her like this reminds me of when she was younger. And nice." Mom said "nice" like Lucy does on *I Love Lucy* when *she's* crying. I felt my face go red. I clenched my fist tighter. Hey now.

There was some more sniffing. It gave me a chance to think. I really had been doing better. At least for a week now I had been nice. I mean, I had said *nothing* about the Elmo slippers since that tragic, embarrassing event was over. And I could have. I really could have.

"I'm better now, Christian. Go ahead." Mom blew her nose. I hoped she had found some tissues. This had to be added to the list.

things to change about MY MOTHER!!!!!!!

24. blowing her nose on inappropriate articles

Now that she's pregnant, she picks up anything and blows. She's so weepy she has to, she says. Laundry has doubled because she grabs washcloths, hand towels and sometimes even the corners of sheets. "I get runny like this," she told me after I asked why she had used the pink guest towel when she was so close to toilet paper. "It happened with you, too. I was runny then as well. Only, this pregnancy is worse."

My mother is an embarrassing faucet, for heaven's sake. Runny. It was disgusting. And now she was sharing her drippiness with a neighbor. Was nothing sacred in our home? Not even our snot?

I had to see what was going on. Eavesdropping was no longer enough.

I moved up a step closer, careful not to make any noise. If only I could watch the two of them.

"I like her, Mrs. Stephan. I think she's great. But I don't know what to do about it."

"Have some melon," Mom said.

"Thanks."

He liked me? Me? My heart gave a little leap of surprise.

There was a quiet moment. I stretched out a bit, trying to make my neck giraffe-like. If only I could get a glimpse of them.

"I know guys aren't supposed to talk to girls' mothers, but I've known you forever too. I think *you're* great. The way you were when you almost burned down the house. Anyone else would have freaked. And my mom is always saying you're easy to talk to. It's true."

"Why, thank you, Christian."

I could just see the corner of the bar in the kitchen. I climbed up one more step and stretched a bit more.

"I appreciate your talking to me, Chris. You're a good kid. And I think Laurie knows it."

Laura, Mom. The name is Laura.

"I hope so. I want to ask her to the movies. Do you think she'd go?"

I leaned a bit farther, angling my body in an awkward *j* shape, my head the dot at the top.

"Do I think she'd go? Well, she is a little young for a date. But if you took a few more people with you and let me take you to the theater and sit in the back, I think she might."

Mom! My mouth dropped open and I got a tiny whiff of my own morning breath. My hand slipped and I teetered for a moment, trying to catch myself. My right arm crumpled beneath me, and with my left hand I made a grab for the banister. But none of that helped.

I fell, my forehead hitting hard on the edge of the top step. I fell right into Mom and Christian's view. "Ow," I said.

Christian looked at me wide-eyed. He seemed to be frozen in place, holding a fork with a piece of melon stuck in it halfway to his open mouth.

Mom gave a slight scream, then a sniff. She grabbed at the green kitchen towel.

I slumped onto the steps as if I were unconscious. I felt quite uncomfortable.

"Laurie," Mom said. I heard her pad over to where I lay and knew that if I "awakened," I'd be eyeball to eyeball with Elmo.

Mom's cool hand touched my cheek.

"She was listening to us," Christian said. His voice sounded muffled, like maybe he was speaking from behind his hands. "I can't believe she was listening to us."

I heard the stool scoot back on the marble floor, and Christian took off, walking fast. "Goodbye," he said.

"Wait," Mom said, and then she left my "unconscious" body lying there on the stairs. "Christian. Don't go angry. She's a Curious George."

"I gotta go," Christian said. "She heard."

The front door opened and slammed shut. At that moment I heard, from behind me, Mary and Maggie coming up the steps.

"Laura?" Mary said.

I didn't move.

"What's she doing?" Maggie asked. "Why is she lying here partway in the kitchen?"

They were right next to me. I felt someone sit down near my feet.

"I think she's faking it," Mary said.

Faking it? Some friend she was.

I heard Mom then, coming back toward me.

"Oh, girls. Good morning," she said. "Breakfast is ready. Go get dressed, then come eat. And Laurie, quit acting, get up and go brush. Your teeth are wearing fuzzy yellow sweaters and I'm sure your breath is bad."

I opened one eye and looked in the general direction of my mother. "Where am I?" I asked, making my voice sound faint.

Mom raised her eyebrows. "You and I have to have a little talk when you're done, young lady, so get going."

I went.

Public Pee-Pee

The first thing I did, before Mom caught me and started our little "chat," was grab my list and add something.

things to change about MY MOTHER!!!!!!!
25. talking about me behind my back

Mom waited till after breakfast for the three-hour lecture on why it's rude to listen in on a private conversation ("But you were talking about me!" "And your point is . . . ?") and why feigning a concussion could be a dangerous pastime ("For heaven's sake, Mom. I had to do something. I'd just fallen into the room where I was listening in on the two of you." "And now we see why private conversations should be kept private").

It seemed like Mom spent every minute of the

next few days telling me why I should be really nice to Christian. At least every minute she was home. The rest of the time she spent at the fitness center taping her commercial. She wouldn't tell me what she was wearing in the ad. All she would say was, "It's going to be a surprise, Laurie girl. But I can't wait for you to see it." *I can wait,* I thought. *I can wait a long, long time.*

One afternoon we were on the way to Dr. MacArthur's office for Mom's monthly checkup when she started talking about Christian again.

"He's a nice boy, that Christian," Mom said. "He reminds me of your dad."

"Christian's not a geek," I said. I stared out the window as we passed through Springville and traveled toward Provo. Traffic was a bit lighter than normal because most of the BYU students were gone for the summer.

"Well, Laurie, neither is your father." Mom smiled at some remembrance. "I'll never forget the first time I saw him."

Oh no, I thought. *Not a memory trip.* I rolled my eyes, then pretended I'd never been more interested in the houses built near Ironton than I was at that moment.

"He was so cute. *Vogue* was here in Utah, doing a shoot in Park City."

"I know the story," I said. I felt kind of grouchy. My forehead still had a red mark on it from where I had smacked the step. Mary and

Maggie had laughed their heads off when I told them what happened, and Mom's lecture hadn't helped any.

Mom didn't stop talking or smiling. "I know you do," she said. "But I like the story. It makes me feel good to think about it."

What it made me feel was weird.

"A bunch of other models and I headed down to Provo because we heard there were places to dance there."

I kept staring out the window. Every other person I knew loved to hear the story of how their mom and dad met. Not me. Not now. Not since the change.

"He was a bouncer at the place we went." Mom giggled. "A BYU bouncer."

What was so funny about that?

Mom seemed to read my mind. "As if an off-campus BYU dance would need a bouncer. We saw each other and it was like . . . well, Laurie, I've never told anyone this, but it was love at first sight."

"You've told me that," I said.

We were in Provo now, headed up University Avenue, a street lined with old shops and trees. The mountains were golden from the summer heat. Mom headed on up the road. She kept talking.

"When I saw your father—and I knew right then he was going to be your father, I just knew I was going to have all girls. That's what I wanted, all girls. Anyway, when I saw your dad standing there in his dark pants and white shirt and tie, I wanted to go ask him to dance."

"And you did," I said.

Mom grinned big now, her puffy cheeks looking puffier than normal with her smile.

"And I did," she said. "I walked right over and said, 'Hey, you wanna boogie?' And your father said, 'Sure.' And then we were dancing so that everybody in the room watched."

"I can imagine," I said. "Especially if Daddy danced like he did at my boy-girl party."

"Now—" Mom said, but I interrupted her.

"Did people really say 'boogie'?" I couldn't look at her when I asked the question, the word was just too horrifying. *Boogie* seemed to me a baby word for something that comes out of your nose.

"You bet," Mom said. Lucky for me, we were at a red light and the car was stopped. Lucky for me also that all the windows were up to keep out the heat, because Mom threw back her head and crowed—and I mean crowed—"Get down, boogie-oogie-oogie. Whooo-oooo!"

I glanced at her, then looked away again. I noticed that my reflection was pink.

Mom turned at Magleby's Restaurant, a place where they know us by name, we come in so often. She started the final bit of driving to Dr. MacArthur's office.

I wanted to look at her, stare at her, will her never to shout such a word in such a loud voice, but I never got the chance. Mom braked hard, throwing me forward. Just one mile an hour faster and I'm sure the air bag would have popped out, possibly killing me. *That* would have made my embarrassing mother feel bad.

"Mom," I said. "What in the world?" My voice sounded angry.

"It's Gary Price's new piece."

I looked at the sculptures that circled the small lawn in front of Magleby's.

"I just love his stuff," Mom said. She put the car in park and climbed out, Elmo slippers and all, to get a closer look. The lunch crowd had gathered on the lawn, waiting for a table inside.

I stared out my window so no one would see that I was with the pregnant Elmo lady. "Mom." I breathed the word and a bit of steam touched the glass. I would have rested my head, but my injury hurt still. I hoped I wasn't permanently damaged.

Mom climbed back into the car. She was huffing a little. "I used to be in such good shape," she said. "Now I can hardly walk and bend over without getting out of breath."

"Hmm," I said. I tried to make it appear that I was not ignoring my mother.

Mom touched me on the arm. "Laurie, honey," she said. "Listen. Christian is a good boy. And he's just right for you. Quinn is . . . he's too old."

"No more lectures, Mom," I said. "Please. You're going to be late." I nodded at the little quartz clock, and she shifted into gear and drove us straight to Dr. MacArthur's office.

I went in for Mom's checkup so I could hear the baby's heartbeat.

"Urine specimen," the nurse said once we were in the checkup room. "Here's your cup." She handed Mom a small Dixie cup.

"For me?" Mom said. "Well, maybe I'm a little thirsty." She faked like she was taking a sip of something, then made a face.

"Gross, Mom," I said. I looked at the nurse, who was grinning her head off. *It's not that funny,* I thought, but I didn't say anything.

"Go do your thing, Jimmey," the nurse said.

"Yeah, Mom." I was mumbling.

"Time to go pee-pee," Mom said.

"Thanks for the news flash," I said. I looked toward a large poster of a huge, naked pregnant woman. You would think peeing in a cup would be a private thing, but even the naked poster woman watched us. Mom waddled into the bathroom, and I waited where her blood pressure would be checked as well as her Dixie cup of surprises.

"Everyone pees here," the nurse said. She smiled at me. "I bet even you do."

"Well, yeah," I said. I felt my face turn red. "Sometimes."

Mom came back in the room and presented the cup like it was a gift. "Here you go, Kathy," she said.

"Hop on the scale."

Mom did.

Kathy, the nurse, moved the weights on the scale. "One fifty-three," she said after a moment.

Mom gave a groan. "I hope it's all baby. A thirty-five-pound baby."

"Blood pressure," Kathy said. And then, "You *are* going on eight months pregnant. This is when the baby puts on all its weight."

"*Her* weight," I said. "The baby's a girl, huh, Mom?" I climbed up on the scale after Mom sat down at a small table, and began adjusting things to find out how much I weighed. The nurse started working to find Mom's blood pressure.

"Whoa," said the nurse. "It's getting up there, Jimmey."

"What do you mean?" Mom's voice sounded funny. I turned and looked at her.

"Let me check again," the nurse said, and pumped up the black band around Mom's arm.

"One sixty over ninety-two," she said, like she was thinking. "Dr. MacArthur can talk to you about this," Kathy said, and hustled Mom into an examination room.

things to change about MY MOTHER!!!!!!!

26. ***public pee-pee***
27. ***saying "let's boogie"—perhaps this word can be stricken from the world's vocabulary as well.***

Boogie Bed Rest

Mom cried all the way through Provo, then through Springville, and into Mapleton. I patted her hand.

She didn't joke with me, not even once, but she did run a red light because, she said, she couldn't see through the tears.

Dad waited for us at home. Mom had just opened the car door when he swept into the garage, scooped her up and carried her inside.

I followed, listening to them talk. Mom was sobbing now.

"The doctor said"— Mom gulped air between all the words—"bed rest."

"Now, now," Dad said.

"Me on bed rest, I don't think I can do it." Mom looked at me over Dad's shoulder. "Who'll take care of Laurie?"

"Mom," I said. "I'm a big girl. I can take care of myself."

"Now, now," Dad said again. He chugged up the stairs like a train. Mom was his weeping cargo.

"He said that this could make the baby come early. She could be here too soon."

That's when Mom broke into such sobs that even my eyes got a little wet listening to her sadness.

When Dad said, "Now, now," the third time, I could hear how sad he was too. Maybe Mom would be great in a commercial. I mean, she was making us all sad, and over bed rest, for heaven's sake.

"Danny," she said. Her words were a little mumbled because her face was pressed into his neck. "I couldn't stand to lose this baby. I've been feeling her move for so many months now. I couldn't stand it."

"Don't talk that way," Dad said. "Kyra's going to be just fine."

Kyra, I thought. *They already named her?* Somehow the name made this unborn baby even more real in my mind. Sure, I had seen her image in the ultrasound. I had also seen her moving in my mother, rolling. Seen what Mom said was an elbow or a foot, pushing like it wanted freedom. But I hadn't realized they had chosen a name for my sister.

"Five babies dead is too many already," Mom said. "This one *has* to live."

"Don't say that," Dad said. "The doctor said bed rest, so that's what we'll do. You have just a few weeks before your due date. Kyra can be born at any time and be just fine."

Down the hall we went, me following behind my parents, so that I almost stepped on Dad's heels.

"Laura," Dad said when he had settled Mom on the bed. "Go get your mother her pajamas."

I hurried to Mom's tall bureau and pulled open her pajama drawer. Mom has a million nighties. She says she inherited her love of nightclothes from the grandmother she was named after, Jimmey Doris. Only, Mom's name is just plain Jimmey. I never met this grandmother, because she died before I was born, but I can't imagine that she had the pajama collection my mother has. Some are flannel things with feet, some are long, silky things with lots of lace, some are just plain cotton with pictures of Winnie-the-Pooh or Peter Rabbit.

"What do you want?" I asked her.

Dad had removed the Elmo slippers and was rubbing Mom's feet. She sniffed now, using the corner of the pale yellow sheet to dab at her nose.

"My Anne Geddes," she said.

I dug through the nightgowns until I found one that was a creamy blue color. On the front was a picture of three babies with purple flowers on their heads. Two grinned and one looked like she had just gotten through crying.

I took the clothing over to Mom, and Dad helped her change. The whole time he talked to her in soothing tones, but I didn't really listen to him. I just thought of Mom, and all those babies she had lost and how I had seen baby Kyra myself in that picture so long ago.

"Laura," Mom said.

I came over next to the bed and stood near her.

"Laurie," she said. "I love you so much." She started crying again.

To my surprise, I started crying too. I grabbed hold of her hand and brought it to my cheek. "I love you, Mom. I do."

I knew right then that those words couldn't be truer. So what if she shouted crazy words in the car? So what even about the Elmo slippers and working in pajamas? So what about her public singing and dancing? Mom had to be one of the best people I knew.

It was two weeks later that Mom got the phone call. I was in bed, asleep, when her scream awakened me.

"Baby's coming," I said. I leapt to my feet, still asleep really, and tried to hurry down the hall toward my parents' room. Somehow my feet got tangled in my bedsheet like it had become rope. My attempt to run nearly killed me. Only the top half of me moved and the movement was in a downward motion. I just missed crashing into my desk.

Mom screamed again.

"I'm coming," I hollered. My heart pounded in my ears and for a moment I thought I might faint for real. I clawed at the carpet and half crawled toward the door.

"Laura!" Mom's voice echoed down the long hall toward my room. "Laura!"

"I'm trying to get to you," I shouted. Was my mother dying? What in the world could be happening? I rolled onto my back and kicked at the sheet. At last it came off one leg.

I got up, threw open my door and started running down the hall, the green-and-white-checked sheet dragging behind.

"What?" With another hard kick I was able to free myself. The sheet sailed like a cloth ball back toward my room, loose ends fluttering.

Mom was sitting up in bed, cradling the phone to her chest.

"Guess what?" Mom's voice was a squeal.

I stood at the foot of her bed now. "Your water broke?" I had seen that plenty of times on TV. Maybe—I raised a trembling hand to my lips—maybe Mom was going to have the baby now. Maybe I would have to deliver it, right here, right here in my mother and father's bed. Ooh, yuck. At least we had plenty of towels. And hot water. And—

Wait a minute, I was not ready for something like this. "Not yet," I half shouted. "You're still too early to let Kyra come."

My mother shook the phone at me. "No, no, no, Laurie."

"You've called nine-one-one?" It felt as if I had become frozen to this spot at the foot of Mom's bed. I might never move again.

"No."

I couldn't make my feet do anything, so I stretched as far as I could, reaching for the phone Mom held. "I'll call," I said. "I'm not sure . . ." Now my tongue was frozen. I couldn't even begin to say, "I can deliver the baby." This was definitely a job for someone trained in more than list writing.

"Laurie." Mom's voice was loud. "That was the fitness center people. Remember the commercial?"

Why would she call them? Had she met a doctor there? Or an ambulance driver?

"This is about the Saturday football game. Do you remember?"

The fitness center? Football game?

"Do you know what I'm talking about?" Mom made the words come out one-at-a-time slow.

A football game? Was she now thinking of taking Kyra to a football game? A newly born baby to a football game? My feet began to thaw. So did my mouth.

"Mom," I started, "you can't take a new baby—"

"No baby," she said.

"No baby?" My voice screeched out of me, and for some reason I fell to one knee. I guess that proves just how scared I was.

"Of course there's a baby." Mom patted her large tummy, then waggled the phone at me.

"There's a baby on the phone?" I asked. I stood up. Both of my legs were shaking, so I wasn't sure I wouldn't fall again. "Our baby?"

Mom motioned me close to her. "Honey. Listen to me." She squeezed my wrist with her hand. "This has nothing to do with the baby. You know that game where they're having old BYU football players come and play for charity?"

"Yeah." I kind of remembered hearing someone say something about it. Maybe it was Quinn. Or Christian. Wait. At my party all the guys had been talking about getting to see Steve Young play ball with Ty Detmer and Jim McMahon. I really hadn't been paying attention, so I wasn't quite sure. I pretended I knew, though, so Mom would get on with the story. I had to find out about Kyra. "Go on."

"My commercial is going to air then. Right. During. The. Charity. Game." Mom shook the phone at me with each word. I dodged it. "Tee-hee," she laughed. And I mean it. She really did laugh out "Tee-hee."

"I thought you were dying," I said, narrowing my eyes. "I thought you were in labor."

"I'm fine," Mom said. The phone was beeping now but still she didn't hang it up. "I've got to call your father."

"You made me lose my dream." This wasn't quite true, but it seemed a fair thing to say, seeing how hard my heart was pounding. I felt all trembly. "Look, my hands are shaking." I stuck both hands out in front of me like a sleepwalker. Neither shook. "People should not be allowed," I said as I turned, "to awaken another person with a scream." I started back toward my own room, scooping up my sheet as I went, but Mom called out to me.

"Laurie, aren't you even a little bit happy for me?"

I turned to face my mother, whose blond hair was messy from a night's sleep. There were dark circles under her eyes. The phone was still in her hand, the one that usually had her wedding band on the third finger. The ring was gone. Mom was too swollen to wear it.

My heart went mushy. "I am happy for you," I said. "Really happy."

And I was. But I still had one more thing to add to my list.

I might not be ready to deliver a baby, but my list-writing skills were as strong as ever.

things to change about MY MOTHER!!!!!!!

28. her screaming like she is in trouble when really she is happy

Promises

From her bed Mom directed the planning of the charity football game party. We had only three days to get ready, which, Mom said, was just enough time to do it right.

She made all the calls, to the caterer, the flower people and a cleaning crew even though the house looked fine. She had Dad and me go to Dillard's and get new bath towels for the guest room near our basement theater. Then she and I wrote out a seventy-five-person guest list, hand addressing each envelope.

"I want all my friends to be here for my television debut," Mom said. "After all, it's been fifteen years." She gave a little laugh, propped up in bed, her hair pulled back into a ponytail.

My guts were doing a tap dance. Mom had convinced me that the only hand towel in the commercial was one that had been slung over her shoulder. Still, I worried.

"I have on a tasteful Rocky Mountain Fitness Center workout suit," she said when she asked me to deliver my share of the invitations. "I hope all your friends can come. It'll be fun."

"You're supposed to be in bed all the time," I said, picking at the lightweight peach-colored blanket that covered her knees. "That's why it's called bed rest."

"I will be. The whole time, right up until the bell rings and the first people start arriving. Then I'll hurry down to my La-Z-Boy recliner and prop my feet up."

"Okay," I said. " 'Cause you know what the doctor said. And Daddy."

Mom smiled at me and reached for my hand. She gave it a little squeeze. "I love you, Laurie," she said.

I smiled at her.

"Now, I'm going to need decorations. Do you think you and Mary could take care of that? You can surprise me."

That sounded fun. "Okay," I said. "Since you promised to stay in bed."

I made Dad do a little promising too.

"No eighties clothes," I said.

"Check," Dad said.

"No dancing."

"Check," Dad said.

"No spinning on your head, no patting Mom's belly, no country-and-western singing, no cowboy boots, no mousse in your hair, no computer talk, *nothing* embarrassing."

Dad stared at me hard. Then he saluted. "Check," he said.

"And no saying 'check,' " I said. "Ever again."

Dad tilted his head, opened his mouth then closed it, and after a moment gave a slight nod. "Ten-four, good buddy. I'll see what I can do."

I just rolled my eyes.

Mary and I spent hours running streamers everywhere, placing flowers around the room and putting up old photos of Mom BM (before marriage). We got lots of balloons filled with helium and let them go so the ceiling was covered in plenty of color just in case someone looked up. We filled three coolers with ice and stuck cans of soda in to get cold. The room looked great.

"I am so excited," Mary said.

"Me too," I said. And I was. Nervous about the commercial, but excited about what would be happening here. About seeing Quinn right here in my very own house.

Mary clapped her hands. "All the guys are going to be here from your boy-girl party, right?"

"Right," I said. "And remember, we don't talk about *the* night. Ever."

"Aye, aye, Cap-ee-ton," Mary said.

"Sheesh," I said. "Have you been talking to my father?"

"No, should I?"

"Absolutely not." Boy, did I mean that. The next thing I knew, Mary might start dancing with my father. He might teach her to break-dance. What a frightening thought.

"Who else is coming?"

I ran through invitations, ticking off the names I could remember from Mom's list, then running high-speed through mine. "And Derek, Maggie, Sam and I think that's all."

And Quinn, too, I thought, but I kept it secret. I hadn't invited Rebecca to come with him because I wanted to have a chance to maybe sit near him, if it was possible.

"Is Christian coming?" Mary asked.

"Maybe." I hadn't spoken to him, not once, since the morning he caught me spying on him and Mom. Until yesterday, every time I saw him, he looked the other way. Yesterday I had given him an invitation, walking it to his door even, the names Quinn and Christian written in my best handwriting on the cream-colored envelope.

"For Mom's party," I had said to Christian. I had stood outside the door to his house, cool air blowing out on me, things smelling a little like spaghetti. He'd said nothing, only raised his eyebrows.

I backed down the stairs. "Hope you can

come," I'd said, lifting my hand to shade the afternoon sun from my eyes. "Quinn, too."

Christian had shrugged, then shut the door with a soft click. It had sounded worse than a slamming door, though I'm not sure why.

Now I said to Mary, "We'll see about Christian. We'll see if he even shows up." And I kind of hoped he would.

Her Exercise Outfit

Dad helped Mom into her La-Z-Boy as soon as we heard car doors slamming outside. He tucked a blanket around her knees and there she sat, makeup on for the first time in days ("I can't let them see me without it!"), hair all done ("What will they think if I don't at least brush my hair?") and in a pretty pink outfit ("I don't look that terrific in my jammies").

"I haven't been up in so long," Mom said, "I can hardly stand the wait."

"Remember, Jimmey," Dad said. "Laura and I will do anything you need us to do."

"I won't risk baby Kyra," Mom said. She smiled like nothing else, her face all lit up. "Being in bed has been such a bore."

"Still, I want you to take it easy," Dad said. He planted a kiss on top of Mom's head.

"I'll not be overdoing anything," she said.

I could only hope this would be true. And about the commercial. I could only hope for a towel as big as a tent. I glanced at Mom. No, a towel bigger than a tent.

Mary was the first kid to arrive.

"Help me greet," I said when I let her in. It was hot outside and the smell of petunias swept in through the front door.

"I love this!" she said. "I love parties!" Mary clapped.

"I know it," I said. "That's because you have your parents and I have mine. Parties at your house are nothing to fear. Don't forget the Night." I did a little bit of a dance, chugging my arms around, trying to look geeky. What I needed was a too tight silky shirt and a sequined glove like M.J. used to wear. Darn my luck for not having those things.

"But Laura," Mary said. "You told me your mom and dad promised not to do anything embarrassing. Besides, even if my parents were embarrassing, and they are, they would never have a caterer show up and do this kind of thing." Mary threw her arms out, meaning my whole house, maybe my whole *life*.

If only she knew.

Mary and I answered the door as Mom and Dad's many friends showed up. It wasn't long before the game was about to start. That's when I saw Quinn come walking down the driveway from where he . . . what was that? From where he and Rebecca had parked.

"Oh no," I said.

"What?" Mary looked out too. "I see," she said. "No Christian. Maybe he'll still show up."

"Yeah," I said. "Maybe so."

Quinn and Rebecca made their way down the driveway, hand in hand. They were still kind of far away when he said something and Rebecca threw her head back and laughed to the sky. Her hair swung around and Quinn reached right over and kissed her a long one on the mouth. It was such a long one that Mary said, under her breath, "Get a room."

I wanted to look away, but I couldn't. The man I loved was kissing someone else. The man I planned to marry, the man I would have five children with, the man I would wear Elmo slippers for, was kissing someone else passionately in my driveway.

"They need to come up for air," Mary said. She sounded a little disgusted. "Have you ever noticed how some people are? They could care less we are here on the porch staring our eyeballs out at them."

"Let's not look anymore," I said, and backed into the house. Mary followed behind and let me close the door. I fell against it and squeezed my eyes shut. There was a pain in my heart. A deep pain.

"Laura," Mary said, and her word came out as a gasp. "Laura." Then her eyes got big. Not big as saucers, like people say in books, but pretty darn close to that. "You like him," she said. "You *like* Quinn Sumsion, don't you?"

"No," I said. And it wasn't a lie. I loved Quinn Sumsion. I loved him.

"You do," she said, her voice full of wonder. "And all along I thought it was Christian that you liked."

I didn't have time to say anything, because right at that moment the bell rang.

"I'll get it. Should I let them in? How about if I tell them to go away?" Mary asked. "How about if I tell *her* to go away?"

I shook my head. "They've been invited," I whispered. "Or at least *he* was. They must be allowed to enter." I felt a bit noble, though there was still that awful pain in my chest.

"Well, fine." She hurried to the door and opened it wide. "Downstairs to the theater," she said, and her voice sounded a bit icy.

I had made my way to Mom's front office, where I glanced around the room and wiped at my eyes. At that moment I was filled with sorrow.

Mary came in behind me. "Laura," she said.

"What?" My voice came out a squeak. How embarrassing.

"I've sent them to the theater," she said. "You okay?"

I nodded.

We stood silent in Mom's office for a moment. I had to change the subject. "She hasn't done any sculpting in a long time," I said when I trusted my voice. "She has one piece partway finished in her studio."

"This party," Mary said. She rested her hand on my shoulder. "Maybe it will make you feel better. Just don't look at the two of them. Hopefully they're way in the back. And maybe Christian will still come."

"Maybe," I said. But now I didn't care. In fact, I didn't even want to be at the party. Of course, I had to be, to make sure that the commercial was right. But I didn't *want* to be.

"Laura," Dad called up from downstairs. "Game's about to begin."

Mary gave me a tight hug. Her hair smelled sweet, like flower shampoo.

"We better go," I said. "Mary, you're a great friend."

"Of course I am," she said. "Now remember, don't even look at those two."

The party was loud with people talking and laughing. Everybody was trying to find a seat to watch the beginning of the game. Most had already dug into the food. I made a valiant effort to do what Mary said, not to look for Quinn and Rebecca, but my eyes seemed to have a mind of their own. I found them both right off. They had snuggled up on the floor with a plate of food between them.

"Great," I said.

"Don't look," Mary said. She turned me away from the crowd. Now I faced my mother instead. Had she noticed that Quinn was cheating on me? If she did, I sure couldn't tell. A group of women stood near her. One said, "Jimmey, you were a beautiful model. These pictures of you are simply stunning."

"Back in the olden days I had perky breasts," Mom said. I spun away, realizing I wouldn't get comfort from my mother. Still, I heard Mom finish, "Thanks to sagging, these are now thirty-two longs." I could imagine Mom pointing at her own bosoms, and I felt glad I had missed that part of the demonstration.

The whole group of women laughed and one of them said, "Ain't that the truth? Nursing and babies does it to you, huh?" The women laughed again.

"Heh, heh, heh," I said, but the laugh was fake. I moved away from my mother, then avoided getting too close to my father. If Mom and her friends were talking about breasts and nursing and other horrible stuff, I didn't even want to know what my father was talking about. That old saying "What you don't know can't hurt you" seemed good advice.

A bunch of my friends, kids that had come to

my boy-girl party and a few others, had pulled up folding chairs at one side of the room. "Let's go sit with everybody," I said to Mary.

She had heaped her plate with food. "We can share this stuff. You get us drinks." I went off for sodas.

The announcer shouted out the kickoff, and the room exploded with cheers when the TV camera found LaVell Edwards standing on the sidelines, out of retirement to coach this one charity football game. Mary and I sat down with our friends.

While I watched the game, I worried only a little about my mother's commercial. Mostly I worried that there was no way I was going to be able to convince Quinn that he loved me and not Rebecca. I could see that.

The commercial started at halftime. "It's on," someone said. And sure enough, there stood my mother in the outfit she had described: the Rocky Mountain Fitness Center outfit. The bright blue, spandex outfit. The bright blue, very tight, spandex outfit. I should never have worried about the towel. Mom had been right about that.

"Yeah, baby," Dad shouted. Everyone laughed.

Everyone but me. At any other moment Dad's screech would have embarrassed me, but he didn't even stand a chance now.

What did it for me was that outfit. That

tighter-than-tight, bright blue, spandex, let-me-see-both-your-bosoms-and-very-pregnant-body outfit. I felt my face drain of all color. The tip of my nose actually felt cold.

I glanced around the room at all the people grinning as the longest commercial ever made was aired on television.

Mom, I thought, looking back at our huge screen. My neck would hardly work. *Oh, Mom.*

On the front of Mom's exercise outfit was a picture of a man trying to lift a huge barbell. The weights dragged downward and the bar arched in the middle as he strained to lift the extreme weight. The problem with it, though, was where the weights ended up. Each side of the barbell landed right on top of one of my mom's huge bosoms. Why, it looked like the the fitness center guy was straining a gut to lift my mother's breasts.

All the blood in my body now rushed to my face.

"Oh no," Mom said, "would you look at that outfit. Why, it looks like—"

I jumped to my feet. "Don't say it, don't say it," I hollered.

Everyone in the room turned to stare at me.

"Say what?" Mom said.

"Don't say anything about . . . about . . . your thirty-two longs."

Mom looked back at the TV, her head tilted like maybe she didn't know what I meant.

"My thirty-two longs?"

"Your thingies and the barbells," I shouted. "How could you do this to me, Mom? How? And for the whole wide world to see."

It was then that I ran. Right past Quinn and Rebecca, whose arms were slung around each other. Right past my father and mother, who looked at me with wide eyes. Right past Christian, whose mouth hung open, practically resting on his chest. When had he come in? The whole group of people, more than seventy of them, watched me run from the theater, and they all appeared surprised. Without a doubt this was not an intelligent group of individuals. As I hurried from the room I heard Mom say, "I meant I sure did look pregnant. What in the world did she mean . . ." And then, thank goodness, I was out of hearing range.

things to change about MY MOTHER!!!!!!!
(when I get the list)

29. her fitness center exercise outfit
30. her FITNESS CENTER exercise outfit
31. HER FITNESS CENTER EXERCISE OUTFIT

Acting Careers

My plan was to stay out in my little playhouse, hidden, until everyone left. Daddy had this place built for me when I was five, and even now I love it, though it's getting a bit small.

"Kyra," I said, once I'd sneaked through my backyard so no one would see me. I hid behind trees till I came to the little gated house. I stepped over the knee-high fence and, ducking, went inside. "Kyra, hurry on here."

I sat on a bed that ran the length of one wall. Things smelled musty. How long had it been since I'd played here? More than a year?

"Your mother, Kyra," I said, looking around the room, "is a crazy. And your father is just as bad. They do goofball sorts of things and wear goofball clothes. They're both goofballs." I wanted to cry, felt I needed to cry, that I *must* cry, but there were no tears.

So instead, I imagined Kyra, small like I had been, toddling around this room, maybe going to sit at the table that still held a china tea set. Kyra looked like I had, the same blond hair, the same big green eyes. In my imagination she sounded like me too.

"They *are* goofballs," she said.

"I'll do my best to protect you from it," I said. "I'll take care of you and we'll come out here when they start acting like weirdos. Of course, that'll mean we'll be here for the rest of our lives."

I imagined Kyra playing with the tea set, picking up a cup and sipping pretend tea from it. "If we're both here, it won't be so bad."

Ha! I thought. I lay back on the bed, bending my knees so I could get on it all the way.

Even if my mother and father had one million children, they would always be horrifying me. People thought Mom's talents were modeling and sculpting. People thought Dad's talent was starting computer companies. Well, everyone was wrong. My parents' talent was humiliating *me*. It was their goal in life. And man, if you asked me, they were succeeding.

I needed my list and I needed it now. If I had it in the playhouse with me, I'd write a thing or two. Maybe when things had calmed down inside—meaning when everyone had left—maybe then I could make a copy of the list and keep it out here. A person could never have too many lists.

things to change about MY MOTHER!!!!!!!

32. her acting career
33. her exercise habits
34. modeling
35. being in the public eye

"Why, why, why," I asked the ceiling, "why did she wear that exercise suit? She was bosoms and belly with a pretty face sitting on top." I squinched my eyes closed at the memory. What had Quinn thought? Now he would never marry me. Rebecca wasn't my worst problem with Quinn. Neither was the ten-year age difference. My mother was my own worst enemy.

"I am twelve years old," I said, "and my life is stinking over. I'll never be able to show my face in public again. Kyra, Kyra, this is what you have to look forward to."

I took a deep breath and let out a "wah, wah, wah" sound, trying to cry. If I could just get this off my chest—no, I couldn't say that, because it made me think of Mom's thirty-two longs with the barbell guy—if I could just make myself feel better, I'd . . . well, feel better.

"Wah, wah, wah," I said again.

It was then that I saw it. A bit of red that was not a little bird. Why, that was a bit of red that looked a lot like the sleeve of a T-shirt.

I sat up fast, the *wah* all knocked out of me. "Who's there?" I asked.

The sleeve quivered a moment, then moved out of sight of the window.

"Who is peeking in on me?" I said. What nerve! What nerve! How could anyone listen in on me during the darkest hour of my life? How?

I leapt to my feet and nearly knocked myself out on the low ceiling of the playhouse. *Thunk,* went my head.

"Ugh," I said.

"Are you okay?" came a voice from outside.

"No," I said. My voice was a moan. "Oh, no."

Christian appeared in the doorway, stooped over so he could come inside where I staggered about, clutching my head, which was surely gushing blood all over me.

I glanced at him. "Am I bleeding?" I asked.

"Move your hand," he said.

I did.

"Nope," he said.

"Are you sure?" And then I said, "How long were you out there? How much did you hear? And hey, wait a minute. You . . . Christian Sumsion, you were listening in on me."

Christian raised his eyebrows. "So," he said.

"So? How can you stand there and say that, all

hunched up in this playhouse? You . . . deceiver. And I'm injured. Are you sure there's no blood?"

"Deceiver," Christian said, ignoring my question. "Listening in on a person makes someone a deceiver?"

"Yes it does, it certainly does." I lowered myself back on the bed. Christian kept standing there all stooped over, blocking the little doorway and the window, too.

"Well." Christian's voice was a low sound. "Well, well, well." He took a step toward me, his finger raised a bit. "Even if you listen in on me?"

I jumped to my feet again, fast as anything, but curved over too. I was nose-to-nose with him. "I did not know you were in my house talking to my mother until I heard you."

"And you listened."

"Of course I listened," I said. "You were talking about me."

Outside, a bird—not a red bird, I'm sure—sang a song. A hot breeze tried to breathe past Christian.

"You are a deceiver," Christian said. "If I am, so are you."

"I had to listen," I said. "I had to. But you didn't. You saw me run out of there." I flung my arm toward my house, nearly jabbing Christian in the eye. He ducked out of the way just in time. "You saw her ruin my life. My whole life."

Now I turned and took three baby steps, till I

was nose to nose with the wall. I heard Christian move too, but I didn't look around.

"I'll never be able to leave this place. Ever. I'll have to grow old here." I raised both arms, and my fingertips brushed the ceiling first and then the walls. "I'm so embarrassed."

Now I could cry. Now I was *going* to cry. Right here in this little room, with Christian breathing down my neck, I was going to cry a lake of tears.

"I know what it's like to be embarrassed," Christian said.

I turned, sniffing, batting my eyelashes to keep the tears back. "You do?"

He nodded. "Sure. I was horrified. I didn't want you to hear those things I said."

Christian and I were so close I could smell the spearmint of his chewing gum. We were so close I could see the dark blue of his eyes. We were so close I could have kissed him right then and there. My heart fluttered. *Oh! I . . . wait a minute. He is cute.*

I looked away, toward the tiny tea set on the little table. "I'm sorry for listening in on you that day," I said.

There was no sound in the playhouse now, except for the yard noises that drifted in through the open windows: crickets and the one bird that kept whistling.

"Well," Christian said. "I'm sorry too."

It was then that I heard the whine of the

ambulance as it came down the street, getting louder and louder.

"Listen," I said.

"Yeah," he said. "It's an ambulance. So?"

"It's coming here," I said. And with that, all bent over, I pushed Christian aside and ran.

Peep Shows

I rushed to the house just in time to see two EMTs hurrying down the stairs with a stretcher. I heard an unfamiliar voice say, "Folks, please back up. We need room to work here. Please."

Mom lay on the floor in the theater with a crowd of seventy-five gathered around her. I had to stand on the buffet table to see this, there were that many onlookers. Christian climbed up beside me.

From my perch I could see a few bald heads, a bunch of kids, a lot of grown-ups, Mary—grinning her head off—Mom on the floor and Dad kneeling beside her. Only my father looked worried.

"Hi, Laurie," Mom said when she saw me above everybody else. "Guess what? My water broke."

"During the party?" I asked, but she couldn't hear me. The crowd was talking.

"Isn't this wonderful?" one woman said.

"And what a day to have a baby. During the charity game with LaVell Edwards coaching." This was a guy.

"I'm so glad I came," said Mrs. Fangle, a lady who goes to our church. "I love a new life."

Then someone said, "I feel faint," right as the paramedics managed to cut a hole through the spectators.

"Please let us through," one of the paramedics said. "People, please let us through." He knelt, crooked, beside my mother. "I need some room to maneuver," and then, "Oh, Mrs. Stephan. How are you?"

"I'm having a baby," Mom said. "A baby! Isn't that wonderful?"

"Yes, ma'am," the paramedic said. He smiled like nothing else. Apparently he hadn't seen the commercial. "I just saw your commercial back at the station. You know, the one for Rocky Mountain Fitness Center?"

By now the second guy had made his way through the group. "Yeah, Mrs. Stephan. You looked fantastic. My wife's pregnant and now she's planning on joining the gym because of you. She called and told me so." He turned to the crowd and addressed everyone. "Only very close friends can be here now. The rest of you leave, please."

No one budged. "We're all good friends," someone said.

"That's right," Mom said. "They're all wonderful friends. Aren't I lucky?" Mom clasped her hands under her chin. "A new baby, a beautiful daughter"—here she pointed at me—"and all these friends."

"I feel faint," a squeaky voice said.

"Then we'll all just have to clear the room," the second paramedic said. "Everybody please leave."

"Aww," someone said, disappointed, as the crowd began to shuffle away.

"That's not fair," Maggie said. I waved to her from the table as she went past.

Mary, though, climbed up beside me, the remains of sliced meats and potato salad at her feet. "You're back, Laura," Mary said.

I nodded, then gave her a fake smile. "I told you the commercial was going to be awful." It was true. For days I had worried her about the will-Mom-wear-a-towel-only problem. I would have been luckier if she had. Why, this had turned out to be a showing, an unveiling, a peep show, for heaven's sake.

things to change about MY MOTHER!!!!!!!
    36. peep shows for paramedics

The room cleared out except for Dad, Mary, Christian and me. And the paramedics, of course.

"Let's get you up and check your vitals, Mrs. Stephan," the first paramedic said.

"I feel queasy."

"Dad?" I said from the table.

Dad looked at me, face white as a cloud. "Hi, honey," he said, then he fainted dead away.

On August 13 at 5:43 P.M. Kyra Leigh Stephan was born, with a revived father sitting hunched in a chair. I know 'cause I was there, standing beside my mom as it all happened. It was pretty cool, especially after they got Kyra cleaned up and wrapped in a blanket. I was the third person to hold her, not including Dr. MacArthur and the nurse.

That evening at about seven-thirty I went home to pack a bag so I could spend the night with Mary, while Dad—still recovering—took care of Mom and Kyra Leigh. All three of them would be home in twenty-four hours.

"I don't want to be long from you, Laurie girl," Mom had said as I walked out the door with Mary's mom.

All the way home Mary and Mrs. Wolf chatted about how beautiful Kyra was (they saw her through the glass) and how lucky I was to have a new sister.

"I know," I kept saying. And I meant it. A sister. A sister for me. A small bundle just for me.

At my house I promised Mary that I'd hurry on over. She wanted to stay with me, but there was something I had to do. Something I had to do alone.

Quick-like I packed a few things, including books, for the night's stay. Then I made my way into Mom's studio. Soft evening light poured in through the windows as I looked at all Mom's art.

There were statues of me and of Noah's ark, animals included. There were statues of girls reading and parents together with a child. And then, on her worktable, I saw her most recent piece, the new baby.

In that warm evening light I looked at the clay statue, so close to being done. All Mom had to do was add a few finishing touches.

I picked up the clay baby and examined her. She was perfect, curled in sleep, just the way Kyra Leigh had lain on Mom's chest before I left the hospital. This statue's eyes were shut and delicate wisps of hair graced the forehead. The lips were parted, almost as if she had just finished eating. Her toes were tiny and had wrinkles.

I thought of tiny Kyra Leigh then. I sure was happy she was around to share the parental burden. We were going to have fun together, the two of us.

"Boogie nights," I said. It just seemed right.

National Geographic Documentaries

I'm not sure what I expected from Mom when she came home, but I can tell you straight up I didn't get it. Or maybe I did.

I thought she would have changed. You know, lost all her embarrassing ways. Birthed a baby and at the same time gotten rid of the way she upset me. That didn't happen at all.

Three days after Mom and Kyra Leigh came home, I found them asleep on the sofa. Mom lay on her back, her head turned a little to the side. Kyra Leigh was curled on Mom's chest, a tiny bundle tucked up tight.

Even resting, Mom's arms wrapped around Kyra Leigh like a protective nest, keeping my sister safe and the two of them close.

Watching her, lying there so still, holding on to that tiny baby, I was filled with love.

"Oh, Mom," I whispered. I wanted to say more, to say how happy I was that she was home and all right, how happy I was that Kyra Leigh was here too. But I couldn't. The words wouldn't come.

With great care I knelt next to the sofa. Using my fingertips to help me balance, I leaned forward and kissed Kyra Leigh's little head. I breathed in deep, smelling her goodness, her babyness.

I rocked back on my heels and squeezed my eyes shut. I could hear Mom and Kyra Leigh's breathing. I felt so . . . so . . . I can't even tell you the word, I felt so right.

Whispering again, I said, "Thank you." This was to God, the guy who had been on vacation during the past few months of my life while Mom horrified me. He must have been watching me a little, though. Here was Kyra Leigh.

I looked at Mom then. I felt so full of love that I thought I'd bust wide open with it. I leaned forward to kiss her cheek. I didn't want to wake her but I couldn't help the way I felt.

That's when I saw the drool. A steady stream of spit that had actually darkened the pillow near Mom's face. My lips were but a few inches away from the slime.

"Gack," I said, falling away from Mom.

Good stinking grief. The woman was nearly forty, and a model. How could she let spit run like that? It was embarrassing. It was sickening. It was . . .

Kyra Leigh stretched then, unballing her body. She made a tiny fist, which she pointed into the air. Then she twisted her back a little and lifted her head. She gave a huge yawn, for something so small, and settled back to sleep on Mom.

"Oh," I said. That had to be the cutest thing I had ever seen in my entire life. "Oh."

"Laurie," Mom said.

"You're awake." Now was a good time to tell her about the drool. But she found it herself and wiped it away with the sleeve of her shirt.

There was a knock at the door.

"Visitors," I said. "Wipe your mouth again. There's some spit right here." I dabbed at my own face to show Mom where. "I'll get the door."

"All right, honey," Mom said. She tightened her hold on Kyra Leigh and sat up to face company.

It was Mary. And Christian.

"Laura," Mary said, and she gave me a hug. "Can we see Kyra Leigh?"

"Of course," I said. "Even *you* can, Christian."

"Oh, thanks," he said, and gave me a smile.

The three of us went into the living room.

"Ooooh." Mary's voice was a squeak. "She's so cute. Oh, Mrs. Stephan, she's so cute."

Again Kyra Leigh stretched. She blinked a few times, then she nuzzled at Mom.

"Here comes my milk," Mom said. "Feeding time. Laura, would you get me that blanket?"

I couldn't move. Surely my mother was not planning to nurse right here in front of my friends. Surely "Here comes my milk" was all the embarrassment I'd be getting for the day. Please, let it be so.

"Here you are, Mrs. Stephan," Christian said. He handed her the blanket, all the while looking out a side window.

"Mom?" I said.

"She's such an adorable baby," Mary said.

"Don't," I said. I leaned toward my mother and whispered, "Not now. No nursing now."

"Laurie," Mom said, a smile on her face, her voice loud. "This is what breasts were made for. Feeding our young." What was she doing? A TV documentary?

"Oh." I turned to my two friends. "Let's go play some basketball," I said. "Quick."

"Yeah," Christian said, and he was gone.

"See you later, Mrs. Stephan," Mary said.

Mom waved to my friends. I hurried after them. "I love you, Laurie."

I stopped in the living room doorway and looked back at my mother. "I love you, too," I said. "Boobs and all."

And I meant it.

things to help my mother do better on

1. *public drooling*
2. *public nursing*
3. *hosting her own NATIONAL GEOGRAPHIC documentaries*

About the Author

Carol Lynch Williams is the author of seven books for young readers, including *The True Colors of Caitlynne Jackson,* an ALA Best Book for Young Adults, an ALA Quick Pick and winner of the Golden Sower Award. Her most recent books for Delacorte Press are *Carolina Autumn,* selected by Bank Street College for its Best Children's Books of the Year list and by the New York Public Library for its Books for the Teen Age list, and *If I Forget, You Remember,* an NCSS-CBC Notable Children's Trade Book in the Field of Social Studies. A four-time winner of the Utah Original Writing Competition, Carol Lynch Williams lives in Springville, Utah, with her husband and their five daughters.